1st 1ou

The Olive of
Minerva
OR
The Comedy of
a Cuckold

EDWARD DAHLBERG

The Olive of Minerva

 OR

The Comedy of a Cuckold

Thomas Y. Crowell Company
Established 1834   *New York*

Designed by Ingrid Beckman

Manufactured in the United States of America

Library of Congress Cataloging in Publication Data

Dahlberg, Edward, 1900–
        The olive of Minerva.

        I. Title.
PZ3.D1374Ol [PS3507.A33]   813'.5'2   75-20358
ISBN 0-690-00697-7

10   9   8   7   6   5   4   3   2   1

To my beloved friend Coburn Britton

With grateful and affectionate
acknowledgments to Nicholas Ellison and
Harold Billings.

With grateful acknowledgment for the
assistance of the Creative Artists Public Service
Program and the National Endowment of the
Arts.

 PART I

Abel regretted everything he had done. Yet he had small hopes, ice-clad stars at the Poles. His Pleiades had already set. But for what? Where was that Lethe'd midsummer ephebe, dead russet leaves swept into the gutter before he had become a lost ravaged man in Limbo? Before he had learned what he must needs see, he had stepped into his fiftieth year. He was unlike the rabble, always pretending to be ready for a hurly-burly with any guinea hen. Now that his head was a nimbus of gray hairs, he was no old child, occasionally knowing his wounds were his guerdon. Each day was a hurricane of stubble. Abel's wildest ill was the wall between him and anybody else. At thirty

he expected much. What a simpleton he was to
chant to Apollo. For years he thought of being
a writer, some kind of outcast motley. Where
was the flamy fennel stalk that he had expected
to use as a quill? Ruby vagaries and canorous
moods are not the granitic perceptions of a
litterateur. A burden of Sidon to his fallow soul,
he admonished himself: "Be quiet, and know
that you are nothing, just Abel." Formerly he
believed the museum streets of the past would
placate him.

What was Abel's predicament? Himself and
the rout. Character is indestructible, and one is
the worse for it as he grows older. Man's
temperament is chronicled in the Orphic
womb, and whatever he does thereafter is
governed by the matrix. A bungler with people,
he cringed as he considered that vast emptiness,
the multitude, though he was big with Void.

The nose masters the face of a savant, a
saint, a wencher, or a usurer, and that is the
most significant feature of genius. But there are
great phallic noses that grasp evil odors, but not
the misdeeds of a foul man. The prehensile
nose is lewd, never tender. Weak-eyed as Leah,
Abel might guess a falsehood though he may

not see it. He abhorred a liar more than the
electrum portal of Hades. One flaw in a man's
forehead and he is done for. A flaccid or gross
mouth is his downfall. For what's in a face a
fool cannot read into it whatever he imagines.

Abel had a starless sky in his veins, and the
pravity of melancholia gorged his head. How
hard it was to be Abel. Little by little every leaf
of him had dropped away, and his arms had
ceased to be a suppliant holm-oak. His features
were ill-placed, otherwise why couldn't he see
what was in front of his nose? He had a
shambling, gawkish gait that signified to a No
Hay Nadan he had been poxed by a daughter of
Moab. What else could he do except sow idle
cogitations by small waters.

A man who states he understands his life
should be confined to bedlam. By now it should
be clear that Abel's brain was as light as the
skeleton of a pelican. Soon as Abel supposed he
possessed a grain of reason, mad cicadas sang
wantonly amidst the danksome shrubs and trees
within him. Every Sunday Abel grayed a little.
Sunday was a spectral no-day, Saturday a
bastard Sunday, and Friday a horrid presage of
an obituary weekend. Abel wished he could

grave the entire seven days. Even when he had
a spell of pleasant tidings in the morning by
even-song he had the vapors. One night Abel
dreamt he was alive, and he wept. Then nobody
is prepared for any occurrence since experience
itself is ever virginal. Was Abel a hopeless
noddy? It's an arcane query, and who can
answer that: he walked, talked, slept, fed,
dunged, and—hence alive—hoped, but
expectations rule us, and Abel, spite of his
vigilance, did not wish to look for anything,
especially marriage, sexual commerce, or a
miraculous "spiced conscience" in a person.

For a long while Abel considered a
Paracelsian receipt for his madness. Unable to
handle his nature, he purchased a charcoal
burner and a crucible which he filled with the
spittle of a crone mingled with Cyphi, two
ounces of juniper berries, seven of myrrh, and
then let them seethe for an hour. After drinking
this receipt Abel felt that he might not be the
victim of some gull-catcher.

He had gone out from that steel and glass
Gehenna, New York. Billingsgate was rife in
the mouths of the street-gamin, the navvy, and
the rabble intelligentsia of the academic dumps

of America. New York was doomed; whores were in all five boroughs and only the seventeenth-century London sign of the boar was lacking to indicate that the apartments were in the red light district. Courtesy was regarded as a malaise of a meacock grout-head. It was time to convert all churches into brothels since the populace was a senseless stock. Now he imagined sandstone, feldspar, hornblende, a roof of honest peasant tiles would assuage him. No tree had cried out of Abel's ribs for a generation. He went to the Antipodes seeking coral hills, sapphire vales, the cerulean daughters of Poseidon. Abel thought No Hay Nada was a hand-wrought Galilean town. Knowing his life was his ruin, Abel expected to have a different existence in the Balearic Isles, in the village of No Hay Nada, though experience is always the same. No lotus-eater, he wasn't pining for a nightshade past.

Abel made one granitic resolve. Commonly, he rambled from one resolution to another, and ultimately forgot all of his intentions. Oddly enough, at least in this, he was similar in temperament to the Majorcan who has as his pole-star an opiate ambition, that is, to do

nothing; better than rushing headlong to the
grave to compass something which in the end
amounts to nothing, anyway. Besides, doing
anything at all is a mischance. Void of
misogamy, he cowered when he considered the
paps; the uterine tribe is spiteful. Abel could
not abide an angular table, a woman thin as an
isosceles triangle, spindled legs of a dour
spinster; not exsanguious, he was no saline
biped either. Since Paracelsian blood is salt,
man in the beginning was a pelagic fish, like
Noah and the fable of the Flood. Abel was air,
dew, a clump of gray locks, not horned or
borned. He would go to a peasant cottage built
of rocks quarried in the Majorcan mountains
and seamed with marl. The Balearics were a
potsherd: Know a people by its terrain. The
patio was covered with fig and almond branches
beneath which he could sit and dissolve his
dunghill chagrins.

Abel now owned seven almond trees near
their senility—although they brought forth
blossoms and sapid nuts—and an apricot tree,
and one-eighth of an acre of thin dreggy soil.
The well water could have cooled his distemper
had he not discovered that it was contaminated

with gnats, flies, and mosquitos. A half hour
after one has quaffed this potion, nourished by
nymphs at the time of Hesiod, he has direful
pain in the small of his back and an abdominal
cramp. A sirocco from northern Africa can
have the like effect.

Everybody knew he had been fleeced by Don
Bartolomé, a Falangist who had murdered
many No Hay Nadans during the Spanish Civil
War. Don Bartolomé told Abel he would not
bring his fruit or refuse through his pelting,
brutal ground unless there was an Afric Etesian
gale or thick, swart weather. Abel was so
overcome by his friendliness that he embraced
him. Duped by a soft winter sky the hue of
wood, Abel also forgot all promises are best
kept in a charnel. As Abel looked over his
almonds, apricot, mimosas and oleanders, he
shed tears. Doubtless he had cozened Don
Bartolomé. Abel loved Bartolomé; he was a
human being, an obsolescent biped in an era of
infinite malice. Besides, man is an automatic
animal, and life is inexplicable. It uneasily
occurred to him that he was mistaken. That was
better than being in the right which was the
cause of sore trouble and madding vexation.

For the natives the sale was a street urchin's jape. Nothing's so much of a rapture to the villager as a simpleton who's been cogged. Whenever Abel entered the *lecheria* or was at the butcher's, he felt their wry glances darting through his back. Without any forewarning there were warts on his two thumbs, a bloat boil on his neck, and an imposthume upon the top of his head.

Abel had a loping shamble that joyed the villagers, and by the time he had walked down Calle Manzana to the dirt café for a small glass of cognac, a troop of fourteen Majorcans were following him.

Next Abel was Don Bartolomé, gorbellied, squab, with patches of Tyrian purple on both chaps; Bartolomé blew out his breath of the jakes, and two Majorcans hastily departed. In a great amaze Don Bartolomé smelled himself, then bit his foul beblubbered lips, and wondered why one odor is worse than another, and if a man gave out an evil scent, was he immoral or helpless.

Bartolomé did his best to forget such malodorous precepts, and presently sat upright, though his paunches still hung beneath his

deceased genitals, in a gown trimmed with
velvet, the usurer's cloth. He couldn't keep his
eyes off burlesque Abel who had purchased a
half-peseta glass of cognac, and loudly
considered the merits of the good, Catholic
waiter, and the *propina* he should lay on the
table. He put down ten pesetas, and the waiter
gave him a low leg, and while Abel was
counting his money, went away with a fleer.
Bartolomé choked, but the mind of the bald
pate of Gaza was elsewhere. Gori, a crooked
stump of a person, a baker, had borrowed two
hundred pesetas at 300 percent monthly. The
baker's wife was a very heavy *criada* who
showed her crumpled drawers, a No Hay
Nadan custom, as she washed Don Tomas'
floor. She was pregnant, but by whom?

Bartolomé was also considering his sundry
fincas which he had stolen from those who had
opposed Franco; he had five *fincas* hard by Inca,
the shoe town, three orchards of lemons,
oranges and almonds in Puerto de Pollensa, and
had sold a hovel on the arm of the
Mediterranean, worth 700 pesetas, for
4,000-pound sterling to an English pensioner.
Abel, thinking he had left the waiter who

venerated the Rood too little, put down on the
table another five pesetas which the waiter
grasped and hurried away. By now everybody at
the café wept with joy. Abel, considering the
goodness of the Majorcan race, understood
Christ's tears of blood in the vale of
Gethsemane, and rising to leave, he declaimed
"Abba, Abba, it is finished." Don Bartolomé
wiped his eyes and nude pate steeped in the
gore of the Lamb with a dirty clout.

A week earlier Don Bartolomé demanded of
Abel the privilege of taking his cart of garbage,
drawn by an underfed burro, through Abel's
patio. Abel paid Don Tomas 350 dollars to
defend him. Don Bartolomé threatened to
report the Abogado to the *Guardia Civil* for
having uttered the sacral name of Franco,
omitting Generalissimo. Abel lost the litigation,
relinquished three metres of his earth, which
gratified Bartolomé so much he had a slight
stroke. Then Abel hired a mason to build a wall
of rough granite; Don Bartolomé began his new
road on the ground that Don Tomas had taken
from Abel. There was a serious balk:
Bartolomé's precious apricot tree that yielded
him 500 pesetas annually obstructed the path.

Besides, the granite barrier could not be moved back one inch.

Bartolomé had a second stroke after which he employed the mason's *obreros,* who owed Bartolomé 4,000 pesetas, to remove the apricot tree without harming its roots. The *obreros,* who abhorred Bartolomé, killed the roots, and the tree gave up the ghost without a murmur.

Then Abel's existence was in the subjunctive mood, always depending on if, or so he presumed. Don Bartolomé, the usurer, was more natural; he did what he was, not what was moral, a human invention the ground of which ofttimes is hypocrisy, self-interest, a voracious crow, murder. Abel wanted to fall into the arms of everybody: Don Bartolomé had a more plain motive: first he wished to loot his neighbor, and if the latter grumbled too much, kill him. Had Abel been familiar with the Hebrew prophet, Isaiah, he might have behaved otherwise, but that is untrue also, since Abel was not by nature sly, occasionally choleric, particularly when somebody stepped on his foot without apologizing; but expunge Abel, the witling, and cite Isaiah: "I will not forget thee, O Jerusalem, unless I forget the cunning of my right hand."

There was another annoy. Fool that Abel
was, he had assumed that learned books were a
balm of Gilead. All hopes hang by the thread of
Ariadne. Seated in a chair on his patio perusing
Urn Burial or *The Compleat Angler*, frequently
he was surrounded by a gaping Majorcan
family. Should he be eating an olive drowned in
oil or picking at a sardine in a tin, or bread hard
as the bole of a tree, he shared his meager
refection with the parents, the children, and a
wily Mallorquin dog. Once he chased a
Majorcan mongrel up Calle Manzana, and the
dog hid behind a tree. When Abel saw where
he was, they looked at one another with much
astonishment.

Abel sauntered through a grove of olives to
quiet the maggots in his spirit. Man's noble
faculties decline as he steps into the fag-end of
his life, but as the olive decays, it is wise as
Minerva. It is fabled that Menelaus came to
Iberia and may have been the first to plant an
olive tree in the Balearics. It is a seraphic
legend, that one myth can obliterate bad luck,
and would have furnished Abel with an
eupeptic hour or so. Shortly, his feathery
inward clime succumbed to a plaguy, underfoot

melancholia. He returned to his roses,
bougainvillea, oleander, mimosas, Tears of the
Virgin, and his workman's hovel.

Abel had long since lost his bedlam
midsummer ephebe; still there were the fumes
of cassia in his everyday flummery in the
hamlet. Each lunar month one might see the
news vendor rolling past the plaza on his
bicycle chanting: "Para hoy, Baleares, botellas,
mentiras, trapos, por la patria, para la tos, por
Franco." Or hear a gray, whiskered man,
barefoot and attired in a ragged mealy shawl,
who had seen his father shot by the myrmidons
of Don Bartolomé, screaming: "La guerra, la
guerra!" The town is a pest house after the
September rains. The wrists of tradesmen are
wrapped in Egyptian flax to truss up their
hands. Wives have a sulphurous rheum in their
brows; the *obrero,* a throbbing megrim.

When the Majorcan is idle, he stands for
hours near the town church, which is opposite
the public latrine. He considers human urine
more salubrious than holy water. When the
gammers are home baking or washing the
seminal denim drawers of the husbands, the
men—jolly as singing cicadas—drink

half-peseta cognac at a hedge-tavern in the
town. Or they sit in wicker chairs hard by the
circulo and play cards. They appear to have
sagacious noses, subtle bones heavily larded
with coarse skin, but vacant Levantine heads.
Like any Catholic, they believe in the
Resurrection without dismissing Man the
Worm. Nature makes no exception to the rich,
the saints, or a bishop—for all must be seated at
the Last Supper of the Maggots. As man is a
superstitious animal, the natives distrust *Puig
Major*, the highest peak in Majorca. The range
of mountains is diabolic, has a ravaging effect
upon the English colony, and is no doubt the
reason why a Majorcan cannot produce
anything except hags. After a foreigner has
sojourned on this blessed isle for six months, he
is impotent.

Every No Hay Nadan who covers his mate
abhors her if she takes joy in it. He deems her
one of a tribe of adulterous Rahabs who will
open the Gates of Jericho to a waiter in a plaza
café, or the rogue who sells water to families
when their wells are dry. Should a woman die
during her menstruous courses, she lies
housebound in state until Thursday, many

hours after the refuse has been picked up. The
stink is so horrid that kindred, friends, and
neighbors leave cakes, wine, orts from the
tables of the rich at the threshold. A common
laborer who has the misluck to expire a few
days before garbaged Thursday is ultimately
carried free of charge to a hole in Tophet and
shoveled into it at midnight. No woman is
permitted to join a funeral procession. She
remains at her abode preparing *sopa
Mallorquina* and baking *ensaimadas,* sweet buns.

The English dwell in Solitario in abstract
kennels on Feline Lane; the grass is an artificial
green pigment. Surgery is their greatest
pastime and their flag a doctor's prescription.
Abel encountered a female Solitarian in drawers
wrought of tin, miasma, sea urchins, and the
stones of a *nispero.* She said, "Thank you" to a
grum apothecary, and Abel was so
overwhelmed by this seizure of courtesy that he
tenderly asked her name and she straightway
shouted for the Guardia Civil.

As for Abel, he had come to this sea-girt
mountainous hamlet neither to kneel before the
Rood nor to acquire horns. Weary of the
vagaries that cankered his pulse, Abel had

decided that he would be a solitary figure. Why
should he make the effort to be lonely when he
already was? Abel, as Rabelais puts it, was an
oaf gat on a knap. His conjecture was feral, and
maybe true: the Hebraic name of that dandy
was Saul, who had expired either of depravity,
the pox and gonorrhea, and whose lecheries
were buried underneath a stone in a Los
Angeles graveyard. People were a disease, and
he resolved to be on guard against his adamant
foe, himself. He was the same as others, only
more desperate about it. Still, it would be a
delight to talk to another person had he not
seizures of emptiness. Can emerald heal the
Cimmerians foggy as the Bosphorus, or the
ruby cure us when we are dead to
everything—Glaucus, the marine green pelagic
god; seaweed; gneiss; a vein of feldspar; the
demise of pensive russet leaves.

Abel descried a throng of people standing on
the pavement of the village composed of the
bones of granite. No Hay Nada looked as if it
had·just received the Last Sacrament. Detesting
the rabble, he rushed towards them to join the
crowd. To further explain this, Abel had been
unable to invent a single incident in the past

two months. Who can endure himself that long? More, a reader of a sort, he recalled Lear's moan, "The world's asleep." Abel roared: "The world's dead."

Now one of none, Abel was watching a funeral procession. He concluded that an Englishman of great worship had just gone to his forefathers. Among the men and women waiting for the sacral hearse were several chits garbed in store aprons made of spoiled rinds of oranges, lemons, apricots, ground glass, bits of iron stoves, and chips of tombstones. A number of rogues were leering at the English, who were gravely chewing varnish, linseed oil, talcum powder, fringes of carpets, pieces of lampshades, and the dregs of mildewed poultices they had pilfered when they visited the sick at the clinic in Palma. The English were wearing suits wrought of fogs and marshes, and shirts of fungoid mushrooms, and the women skirts of sewage water and inspissated shoes that once were the skulls of criminals who had been strangled. No one entered the abode of a Solitarian without being fumigated with creosote. The Majorcan rustics were wearing up-to-date electric drawers. They

were acolytes of the age of shame which is
universal; when the batteries are exhausted, the
drawers fall down to their feet, and they are
naked.

Abel expected to espy a priest who was
expiring as he walked. Wrapped around his
neck was an albic stole concealing his jet black
habit. His aged mien was a plethora of anguish.
Now and then he paused to kiss the feline
sphinx which he held aloft.

The hearse that rolled along the cobblestones
was also used for the collection of garbage. The
funeral wagon was decked with geraniums,
hydrangeas, margaritas, chrysanthemums,
Tears of the Virgin, lumps of spinach, spikes of
celery, imported mandrakes from Haran, and
shrubs of whortleberry piebald with cakes of
salt, sugar, and cinnamon. Drawn by a pair of
scrannel burros which, frightened by so heavy a
funerary parade, discharged steamy urine or
warm manure, the mortuary coach was followed
by workers who carried a bag of Egyptian
cotton into which was dropped the
hand-plucked ordure. Inside the hearse was a
silver casket containing the holy corse, a
deceased, lavender-blue Persian with orange

eyes that was stuffed with mummia and embalmed.

Behind the hearse and pickers were four altar boys, each holding a tabby on the leash. Unbedded wives, spinsters with cats that nuzzled at their naked dugs, and drossy, spado-bachelors kept a number of paces back. Amidst them was a mingle mangle of nuns, those mummified dolls of mercy, with noses that fell below their mouths. They skulk to mealy cells that smell of the incense of moles. Never nubile, their parents offered them to the Church. Nearly every mother and father had an imbecile daughter, or one with a goiter, crippling arthritis, or asthma. The clerics were not able to disguise their horror of these womb-less cretins.

The cat necropolis was situated in Solitario where the foreign colony had settled. Those who filled the graveyard came with wet eyes, brooding on headstones with sundry epitaphs:

"Here lies Abraham of Ur, a prolific Patriarch."

"This is my deceased Shem who warmed my sheets in blizzard, rain, and sleet, and eased my rheumatism."

"Hallowed be the Sublime Ghost of
Nebuchadnezzar, whose forefathers were Kings
in Babylon."

"May Christ guard Miriam, a descendant of
the Prophetess, who fingered the timbrel, and
was more steadfast than the hedge sparrow,
Man."

There were countless slabs, some humble
stones, purchased by a pack-penny father,
others of a rare imported marble—in the shape
of a tom, a stray, a poodle, a hound, a setter, a
terrier, or a dachshund the pigment of
excrement.

The English hired mourners. Four to five
priests had been paid fifty pesetas each to give
the ceremony a Christian air. The padres, quite
spruce, wore tonsures the size of a peseta, since
they declined to shear their locks, thick and
curly as Absalom's. If one by chance looked on
an agynary crook-backed sister of the Church,
he crossed himself and lowered his eyes.

In a trice a mucky rain fell, which the
assembly considered a sign of the displeasure of
the Father, the Son, and the Holy Ghost. The
old, faltering padre was shaking a censer, which
he handed to a thurifer eleven or twelve years

of age. He seated himself on a brown stone covering a dachshund. A crumpled, dim-eyed crone, mistaking the rock for ordure, pulled him up and wiped his sacral vestments with her carcase-petticoat. The cleric, fatigued and mumpish, scolded her, saying that a woman of her burdensome years should return home and mundify her morphewed sins.

A small horde of men and women had fallen into a vehement argument regarding the gender of the defunct Persian. One alleged the coffined cat was male, which brought a cry to a hag, the buckler of the deceased brute, who claimed she had never known sperm. Others insisted it was a castrato.

The downpour curdled the slime, and the assembly began to disperse. A Majorcan boy with a swollen, dotard head, held a tin box in his hands, divided into three sections, one for bread, the second for centimes, the third for his burial. The priests gathered about the altar boys. None could find fault with these austere ecclesiastics who kept their vigils, said their prayers and vespers. It was the custom of novice fathers to buy a handsome boy as a catamite. They claimed the fee of two thousand

pesetas would be used to re-edify a cloister in
Palma.

There were murmurs among the populace,
but who could blame the immaculate brethren
who had never broached a female vessel,
though on occasion an alcoholic or deranged
monk was known to have covered a wife, aunt,
or sister.

The young priests venerated the pubescent
pathic, anointed with frankincense and garbed
in expensive raiment. The Majorcan
ecclesiastics were no different from pagan Zeus
who had a Ganymede.

The procession had ended. None could see
any sin for attending the cat ceremony. Those
who suspected the Logos, the Gnostics who
charged it was the Word that had been
crucified, would not have desecrated the
adoration of the cat and dog, an antique ritual in
the River Nile Valley which the Christians had
translated into the legend of Jesus. Although
the feline funerary services were a trivial
Catholic cavil, but much of a marvel to the
Majorcan as a pilgrimage to Compostello, their
xenophobia never ceased.

Without foreknowledge, Abel began to

eructate. Overcome by this mishap that he had conceived, he also began to sneeze. Is each man who pretends he has a will responsible for his disasters? Certainly there is a scruple of evidence in this axiom.

Abel always carried a feather in his waistcoat which he used to tickle his nostrils. This he had learned from Aristophanes in Plato's *Symposium.* Soon as he ceased irritating the inside of his nose with the feather, he ceased sneezing and belching.

Then he began to cough. A repulsive experience only when somebody else does it. Abel could countenance his own bowels, but he could not step upon human ordure in an alley or hallway without being queasy. Obviously he was crucified the whole day. Should he see loathly matter around the corners of one's eyes, Abel swooned. How disgusting it is to watch a person choking on a bread crumb. The religious adore the Sangrail, but would he have drunk Christ's blood? Man is often void of ruth which makes the Nicomachean Ethics dross. It is odd that the Ethics should bear the name of the child of Aristotle's whore.

Although of the opinion that the descendants

of Chiron and Hippocrates were a band of
thieves, Abel bent his way towards the office of
a Mallorquin doctor on Calle Jesus. Why
should Abel see a mountebank. He himself was
a spagyric apothecary of pellets.

Presently he was standing before El Medico
Muchas Pesetas. Abel's mizzens, poop, and
foremast were broken in pieces. He offered El
Medico his hand, which the latter, a devotee of
the goddess Hygeia, declined. Perhaps it was an
ambiguous gift, or the doctor didn't want to
catch Abel's germs. But whose were more
essential to health—El Medico's or Abel's?
Wavering, Abel considered going back to his
hewn-rock dwellings to bandage his leaky
disposition with clay, splinters of bark, sorrel,
skins of persimmon, oakum.

Abruptly El Medico requested, "What can I
do for you?"

"Sir, nobody can do anything for anyone.
Each must carry Job's faradel upon his own
back." Then Abel added, "Maybe you could
repair my character."

"Which part?" he queried, his mind
elsewhere.

Abel went on: "There's something else

troubling me, a sorrow in my lower colon called Sunday; Sunday tumors the brain and grieves the intestines. Maybe one might repair that charnel chink in the week as Charon caulks his dinghy making for the shores of the Styx with weeds, darnel, sedge, pebbles of the shingle, and seaweed."

El Medico: "Only a man with a sickly disposition would bolt this Gnostic anathema. Either you answer me plainly or go! How many Sundays are there in your week?"

Abel: "There's the bastard Sunday called Saturday; soon there will be seven oafish Sundays in a week."

El Medico: "Can't you sit on the Lord's day?"

Abel: "Only in the privy, sir."

El Medico: "What do you know of yourself?"

Abel: "I've never made his acquaintance."

El Medico: "You realize you have a throat and a neck."

Abel: "Oh, yes, a pimple on it makes me peevish; otherwise I'd never know I had a neck."

El Medico: "Are you you or somebody else?"

Abel: "Had I a smaller foot I'd be morbid as foetid Avernus. Were it long I wouldn't be so nervous though greedy."

El Medico: "Ah, foot! Chilblains, bunions, blisters, calluses."

Abel: "My left foot is dull-witted, a slug two kilometers behind my harebrain." Suddenly Abel exclaimed: "I like you enormously." Tottering, El Medico feared Abel might fall into his arms and so he kept him at a civil distance. El Medico knew that foreigners were a crew of noddles come to Majorca for the cheap peseta, a meal a vagabond peregrine could afford, ordinary wine at two and a half pesetas a liter, and a town seasoned with antiquary centuries.

Unable to restrain his exuberance, Abel asked, "Do you suppose you could physic my fallow intelligence? I have a horrid affliction called sleep shaped like Persephone's grum visage tossing to and fro on a wild darkling sea."

"What ails you? Let's waste no time."

"Myself," Abel assured him. By now they

were diagnosing one another. El Medico had an artichoke nose and swollen chaps resembling the scalding house nowadays known as the surgery. He felt Abel's pulse and put his ear, a crumpled Mammon wallet, against Abel's heart. Abel started to leave, but El Medico roughly grasped him by the shoulder.

"What else hurts you?" he rasped.

"My pains are travelers. Maybe all that's the matter with me is a few pounds of stupidity."

"Take aspirin three times a day, and two before retiring. Does your head trouble you?" El Medico demanded.

"Never, except when I think about it."

"You have an odd smell about you. You've eaten something that's upset your stomach."

"I've been eating my miseries all morning. My bones are a rubbish heap which herbalists claim nurses purslane. Grief makes me smell bad."

"I'd suggest you cease sitting next to yourself. Maybe a small incision in the abdomen would make you more congenial. Are your arms of equal length? If one is shorter than the other we can correct that in my surgery."

"You're going to abbreviate one of my arms

to improve my disposition? What of my bad
nerves which make me a simpleton with frigid
people?"

El Medico's tumid nether lip fell. "Do you
get along with yourself or people? Does your
furniture intimate ill luck for you or engender
black humors or sciatica?"

El Medico: "Do you prepare for a visit?

"Before calling on anyone do you use
purgative rhubarb?

"Have you ever had a good experience?"

Abel: "Offhand none that I can think of."

"Let us momentarily return to your
furnishings in your room. Why are you at odds
with your chair?" El Medico conjectured.

Abel: "Although my chair and I live together
it is as beside itself as I am.

"I am unsteady on my feet whenever I
encounter anyone. Frankly, I'd prefer to live
with myself, but I too am another person, and
so I'm never alone."

El Medico: "Something I cannot fathom ails
you; is it acedy? Why not sit upon a fricatrice, a
tomb seventy to eighty years of age; that might
relieve you of that burden, your other self.
Have either of you met?"

Abel: "No, sir, but coition is a ruse according to the inflexible laws of Nature. Though the male and female gender, each is wholly preoccupied with his private sexual operation. One and one is immutably one. The libertine or the paramour is the most exact sensualist. He exquisitely molds and shapes each of the senses as a lapidary cuts and polishes a gem."

El Medico: "So there's nobody else except you in this world?"

Abel: "No one I can recall. If you called me somebody, wouldn't that be mildly contrary to solipsism?

"Should Hesperus, one of the candles in the firmament, be visible, may I chew the flesh of a calabash or eat a colycinth, the bitter apple, as an antidote to any agreeable anticipation. To make sure I'll not be decoyed by Hope, every morning I'll moisten my craw with dry water, nibble bran, cracknel, and the marrow of a fir branch."

El Medico's head was asleep on his chest. Brusquely awakening he unintentionally roared: "You're a disease shop! A museum of ills. From Monday through Friday drink a pottle of

turtle's blood, and two egg yolks lightly
streaked with the dim saffron sun of daybreak.
Don't associate with anybody unless you don't
care what happens to other people.

"I'll prescribe the phlegm of a fen, a bit of an
ailing pond, alum combined with fuller's earth,
as a sedative to your nature. Mercury, the
Mater Dolorosa of all metals, oft quiets the
bedlamite."

Abel: "I could lay the fillings of lepry Diorite
in a mortar and pound them with a pestle to
strengthen my flaccid will. I cannot finish what
I set out to do without starting something else.
Does that prove I'm an unsuitable person in
this world?"

El Medico: "You'll be a nuisance in the
other world, too."

Abel: "Several unlooked for raindrops a
zephyr during the summer solstice are likely to
provide me with a drachm of doom. Was I born
to boggle good luck?"

El Medico: "You're a fardel of hopeless,
ruined nerves; some element in you is
egregiously dumpish. You're a dungeon of
hypochondria. Even Galen, distraught and
senseless since he couldn't have glued one

nerve to another, would have sent you to the ossuary."

Abel: "What should I do?"

El Medico: "Don't do it."

Abel: "Do what?"

El Medico: "Anything. Life wouldn't be bad as it is would you be courteous enough to leave it.

"Just let me be. I'm overwrought. This is my penultimate physic: Take a few crumbs of sowbread, sundry insults, to truss up your weak character. Don't see anybody; since you can't handle yourself, how in Christ's and Apollo's name will you mangle two of them."

Abel: "I importune you. Please don't be too irked with me. How is it I'm touchy though I don't have any feeling. True, I'm shaken up by a splay-mouthed gutter-blood's fleer who hates me because I'm not somebody else. After such a misadventure I come down with a canicular fever. What's your opinion? Should I swallow my own saline spittle mingled with the boiled leaves of the juniper?"

El Medico: "By now all my opinions are graved. Please give me hartshorn to inhale."

Abel: "I must disclose to you my evil

encounter: A ruffian who knocked me about as
he jostled through a rabble of ninnies paid no
heed to me when I apologized to him. That
pained me the whole day long. Your diagnosis
is extremely acute: No matter what I do I am
dirty and soulless for having done it. Once I
lent a scrub acquaintance 1,000 pesetas; I was
miserable for days because I imagined I was a
good person. That gave me such a nasty taste in
my mouth, a deed of kindness I garnered up
from a precept in the Book of Proverbs.
Furthermore, I had shingles that girdled my
navel. I'm ashamed of anything I do."

El Medico: "You have the mewling nights
and the sour pukes of a baby-man; what may
wean you from the hard, filthy udder of your
sleep. Everyone had bad dreams which he
forgets are his life. This cannot concern you,
but since everything you say is tasteless,
nothing seems too irrelevant: 'No man can
escape his sins though a wicked spouse is to
blame for them.' Why am I speaking so to an
unborn benedict?

"Go to your *casa*, grind seven granules of
copperas, joined with small wood of the shitah
tree and a tablespoon of a saddlebacked hill.

You will then presume you're a whole person.
This may embolden your sacrum as it did
Osiris. Farewell. My wristwatch, our Blessed
Lady, informs me you must go. If I see you
again, which I pray will never occur, do not
expect to be foraging among my pottles instead
of employing my time on patients responsive to
treatment.

"Do you understand women?" So infectious
is a dizzard that El Medico had forgotten he
wanted above all to be rid of him. The
meanwhile he was reckoning his fee on the
fingers of his hands, and then he removed his
shoes and socks to be certain that for such a
cock-brained visit Abel would not cheapen his
customary charge.

Abel: "O El Medico, everything is too much
for me, whereas my day of nothing is a yoke of
endless tedium."

Another divagation eased El Medico's own
spastic bowels; but he returned to the same
unanswerable query: "Do you understand
women?"

Abel: "How can I since I have no vulva."

El Medico, his mind still elsewhere: "Stand
on this scale so that we may see how many

stone of embicility you weigh. Though you're
unusually exsanguinous, a sharp quip frets you
for months since you never had an epigram to
vanquish your opponent, who can cure a
phlebotomy of your squeamish identity. Eat a
carrion hen not trod by a cock for your pipe of
nonsense."

Abel: "Is there any other kind of sense?"

El Medico: "I'd better fee you. And never
come back. Remember, he who hankers for
what is gone is a pillar of salt; only a lazy
lotus-eater aches for any past, the nemesis of
Aristotle's *Praxis.* Besides, you're dead already.
But I never met anybody alive so ridiculous as
you."

Interrupting him, for Abel found no receipt
so healing as a digression, "What's your
opinion of that hogshead of liquids and sundry
solids, Franco?"

Doctor Pesetas crossed himself, said the
rosary, and genuflected.

Abel: "The Generalissimo is a frugal feeder,
and gulches out what he ate the night before to
quicken his appetite for breakfast. Since the
workmen murdered all the fowl on the isle to
supplement their wretched *sopa Mallorquina,*

Franco's matutinal snack consists of
twenty-four imported sparrows, eighteen gulls
from Albion, a basted osprey adorned with
lizards, piebald with a topaz-colored capon, and
a crate of eggs in a trencher, and, in order to
have the courage for his noonday refection, he
takes a clyster so that he can guttle a shoal of
herrings, nine platters of celery smeared with
gills of a gudgeon, and ten delicate
Mediterranean sole. Positively indifferent
towards supper, he eats seven dishes of *paella*
with frogs' legs, a gallipot of Moly. Though he
tips the garotte of an *obrero* he is garbed in a
commoner's jerkin. For dessert he has a great
liking for hare's flesh garnished with
horseradish. Spite of this frugality, he's a
gulligut friar of the peseta who cannot mount a
horse without the aid of five grooms and his
chambermaid. To his credit he drinks no water;
in Mallorca during the Civil War a soldier
washed his face in wine (water was so scarce)
before applying the razor to it."

Abel asked, "Is it true that after coition one
does not require a diuretic? Or would you
suggest it is best to walk along the marshes of
Cadiz where the teal and widgeon feed? And

why is it that it takes a long time to prove
nothing?" Then Abel remembered: "I came to
have my character mended."

"Is it that bad?" El Medico asked. He
ruefully shook his nude glabrous pate. "Champ
a tallow candle along with a costermonger's
moldering drawers, soaked in vitriol; that
should harden your irresolute nature."

El Medico: "Let me see, 500 pesetas for
consultation; 175 for coughing in my face; for
exhaustion of my scales, 250; 125 for wear and
tear of the chair; 1,000 pesetas for your
blaspheme. Did you ever savor the Sangrail; the
maculate aspersion of Generalissimo Franco is
sacrilege. Either this is orgulous paganism or
you're an insatiable sot. For your latter
complaint Amethyst can cloy your incontinent
thirst for cognac."

Abel: "Perhaps it's just rheumatic ignorance.
Suppose I have insects in my head; could not
fleawort have cured Plato who died of a louse
disease? I'm thin-headed. But is that fatal? I
don't care to be uncivil, but where is your
dungparlor?"

El Medico: "Next door to the morgue. As
matters stand, you can enter either. One

hundred and twenty-five pesetas for the deposit of your stool."

Abel: "Is there not a uterine connection between your clinic and the spittle? But I'm still here for I changed my mind."

El Medico: "You were thinking of it, and I have to charge you for your apocryphal excretion. Had you done what you considered doing, you'd be quite normal. Two hundred pesetas for your flux of incertitudes."

Suddenly El Medico turned to Abel: "What did you do yesterday at noon?"

"Sir, I can't recall what I did five minutes ago."

El Medico was still counting, but again he questioned Abel, "Have you any friends?"

"I am fearful of anybody who was ever wombed."

"Don't you have any relatives?"

"Well, there's Aunt and Uncle Jeremiah Little, that is, Mr. and Mrs. Little. And their daughter, Pox Little. And her brother, Villain Little. But I don't see them because, though they died a generation ago, they still allege they're alive."

El Medico: "Everyone except an assassin has someone in this earth."

Don Pablo Williams, a spruce ninety-two and whom Abel visited several times, just had a stroke. Funeral cards were already in every shop, and the storekeepers were overwhelmed with rhapsodic emotions. Don Pablo was the richest man in No Hay Nada, and his credit was spotless. Aside from his abstruse wealth nothing stirred up the populace as a burial parade. He never paid any bills, but instead left pieces of his legacy to those who had his infinite devotion. There was also jubilation because it was said that he would be baptized and, before he was given extreme unction, become a Catholic.

Abel passed the public latrine that stood over against the church. Outside it stood an idle geck and an outcast tatterdemalion half-wit engaged in the jobbing of putrid rags of town gossip.

Father Moses Rodriguez y Caracol was to administer the last rites. It was whispered that Father Moses had a pottle of Judaic blood in his veins. He was also notorious for practices

expected of a laic lady killer. He had run off to
Alicante with a plump widow from the English
colony—taking with him the chalice, ciborium,
thurible, candlesticks, all gold. Some held this
was scabby rumor; others blamed a dowd in
Solitario of satanic presbyterianism. A No Hay
Nada seer declared a truthful person wearies
one unto death whereas a false man is an
amiable companion whose defects are gullish
and kind.

A troop of backbiting scoundrels asked
which wencher was going to confess whom?
Father Moses had already blessed the Don's
house, his orchard, and his three burros.

The Don's demise was expected hourly.
Father Moses arranged his face to be suitable
for a midwinter cemeterial occasion. When
Dolly Patch, shrunk with cognac, thought he
could espy Father Moses he assumed that he
ought to genuflect. For last rites, it was opined
that Father Moses used vegetable oil in place of
the sacramental olive oil prescribed by the Holy
See; and that money allowed him for the olive
oil he pocketed, even borrowing the dregs
which the workmen smeared on their loaves.

Presently he was on the patio with Don

Pablo's brother, Dolly, the dwarf with azury scambling eyes, but he paid no heed to his tears, nor was he impressed when he saw him wringing his hands and crying aloud: "Death, death! That it should even happen to me!"

Father Moses, who had flaring Afric nostrils, a hybrid nose, part Hebraic, the rest Arabian, and a hungry gait, gave him a cross-grained glance: "Who's dying, you or your near kin, Don Pablo?"

Dolly, weeping, said, "Does it matter, Father?"

The priest answered, "Yes! To him, but perhaps not to you!"

Father Moses entered a cavernous, dark bedroom. Evidently Don Pablo had been a traveling man, for he noticed a chest from Ceylon, a Mexican blanket, an Aztec image of Quetzalcoatl on a bare wall void of a crucifix. He crossed himself hurriedly and commenced: "Do you wish to leave this hedonic world a devout and true Catholic?"

With short, huffing breath came the reply, "Yes, good Father."

Padre Moses anointed his forehead, eyelids, temples, and nostrils with the rancid dregs of oil, and being a distraught man, added hebenon and oak galls.

"I hear you've been an indefatigable fleshmonger."

"Ah, good Padre, gossip is a traveler; not Caesar nor Nero, who introduced the forced march, could reach an enemy more quickly than hearsay. However, I am too close to the grave to conceal my brutish faults. Sure, I was a skirt-chaser, a fleshy josher, and I had a music-hall voice, but I squandered my sperm, and all the tones are clean gone out of my craw. Once an irate husband put a knife into my back for assuming I had inhaled the odoriferous perspiration of his spouse's blouse—and I bled voluptuously. More, I admit that having stepped on a nettle I felt a carnal throb as I probed and disinfected the wound in my foot. Handling a doorknob or key overthrows all my honest precepts. Inanimate objects are as ticklish as a woman. I do not deny that an orchidaceous shift peeping below the dress of a vixen did not foment an incontinent turpitude, but I immediately rejected this inflammatory humor with revulsion. Or had I by mischance descried a buxom Corinthian leg I must divulge

I was conquered by a pining hunger for this minx until I loathed my stygian tumult and, in a trice, was indifferent to her succulent body. Do not suppose that I look for such wily and unlooked-for sensations without Biblical wrath."

"These are venial sins, and your opposition to them symptoms of salvation. You oppress your nigh carcass heart overmuch. Besides, there is nothing in Holy Writ that says inanimate objects may waken concupiscent aches. Should one be taken with the falling sickness, and then suppose he is able to cohabit with a chair, a doorknob, a window ledge, or a lexicon, that's just a cock-brained fribble. Don't be vexed or fall into dudgeon lest I purge you with hedge-hyssop."

By now the expiring man, heated by his naked disclosures, threw aside blanket and sheet. He was wholly attired but like a tattered, wandering beggar. Father Moses gaped at the rich man's slop-clothing with considerable astonishment and this madding spectacle almost raised gravel in his craw. "Why does an affluent man garb himself in vagabond trousers and a

penniless jerkin too feeble for nourishing a
moth?"

"My humble exterior is a Vulcan's shield for
warding off the voracious trull, and the cogging
ruses of the confidence man."

Momentarily Don Pablo coffined his small
misty eyes while mumping his apprehensions.
"There is little left in my exsuccous head
except a Catholic shroud."

The Padre was visibly impressed.

Don Pablo: "Most Holy Father, knowing
nothing of the public stews or the amorous
stings of a leman, I've always assumed the
conceit of a layman, mind you, that man should
hoard his inly force for prayer and
meditation—and if I err and am profane I avow
I am contrite, and if I'm a liar may my stool be
costive and hard as February ground."

Father Moses: "The Church of Rome
declines to think a pious man dungs; regrettably
it happens, but such laic matters are best
unspoken. Still, I must perforce bless your
Catholic asceticism.

"We must overlook the droppings of dirty
starlings, the incontinence of the short-lived

sparrow, an undeniable proof of retribution."

The Padre champed his sapless lips to excogitate the famed infinite plenty of Don Pablo: "Since the Lord God is the Guardian of the kosmos and its gold, silver, platinum, all ore, the earth, property, houses, and as the poor are the wealth of the rich, tell me, and don't dissemble, how did you come by your immense investments in Spain, England, Indochina, the Antipodes, and the New World?"

Don Pablo declined his head, his eyes moist with astral humility: "Beloved Father, I admit I've scambled up money and am now too ill-skilled to reckon the continents and seas I possess, but as an act of penitence, *Abogado* Antonio Mentira has drawn up my testament and all writ without multifarious clauses or opaque, illiterate legal quibbles that assures the Church of my gold mines at Potosí, all arable earth surrounding Lake Titicaca for monasteries, five million pesetas for hospitals, a million for a Memorial Don Pablo Williams Foundation, whose prodigious resources will be used to establish committees of scholars of lechery and to make annual reports suggesting the alleviation of this incurable malady; an eye,

ear, and nose clinic will be erected in Palma for
paupers and unfortunate maidens big with
child; twenty alms rooms for spotless aged
crones; a Don Pablo Williams Apothecary for
the poor who have been swindled by
quacksalvers of medicine; ten million pesetas to
be set aside to exile pettifogging lawyers,
speculators in bread, butter, milk; a sanitorium
for impotent brothels who beseech the Catholic
Church to proselytize them."

Don Pablo fell into one of his spells of
aphasia, and recovering asked Father Moses
whether he had impregnated one of the wives
he had blessed for the customary five pesetas
the Church exacted of the hungry *obrero*'s
family.

Father Moses shook a long splenetic finger at
him and Don Pablo, oblivious of his own
paralysis, was prepared to kneel and beg
forgiveness of the Virgin Mary. Once more
Father Moses reminded him he was a humble
cleric and hardly the mother of Christ.

Father Moses' next query was: "Be simple,
my aged boy, have you ever had black Judaic
seizures?"

Don Pablo sheepishly replied: "O Father,

don't all of us pray to fables, Isis, JHVH, Zeus,
The Word, according to the Gospel of John?
More, the gnomes who wrote the Scripture had
no ballocks. I'd rather civet my imagination
with anise, myrrh, frankincense and camomile
than Matthew, Mark, Luke, and John."

Father Moses' ire was a surging tide: "Are
you Anti-Christ? Thus your impious Rood is
Bread, Lucre, and Usury. Had our Pope in
Rome heard such heathen conceits, straightway
you'd be in the *Index Purgatory.* I can't shrive a
bombastic pagan alchemist. Say, is it the Cross
or a Paracelsian crucible?"

Don Pablo: "I'm an inherent bungler; I
kneel, and rub my sputum upon your devout
brows.

"What's happened to Señora Bernadina
Ruido?"

Father Moses: "Muerto."

Don Pablo: "I saw her yesterday afternoon."

Father Moses: "Aged infant, what has time
to do with death? Besides, the Angel of the
Apocalypse says there are no weeks, months, or
years in Paradise."

Don Pablo: "Señor Tomás Basura hasn't
visited me for a fortnight. Why?"

Father Moses: "Muerto."

Don Pablo: "Then there's Jaime Bauza, the iron-monger; not a word from him in a month, and I liked all of his defects."

Father Moses: "Muerto."

Don Pablo: "Is everybody dead?"

Father Moses: "Why not: give me one good reason why anybody should want to be alive. I'd die right now, if the Catholic Church would permit it. And you, too, are a balk. How can I expire, if I must perforce give you extreme unction?"

Then Don Pablo, admitting he had never given a tithe of his brave intellect, went on: "In my legacy there is a provision for board and lodging in an abbey that will contain 2,000 centenarian cuckolds and one wittol."

This time Father Moses raised his thick, furry eyebrows and his long bugle nose as if he were about to blow his astonishment through it. With reverence Father Moses asked: "How is it that cuckolds almost attain the great age of the Hebrew Patriarchs, Abraham and Joseph?"

Don Pablo, rather shaken by the ecclesiastical deference of Father Moses towards him, replied: "Some cuckolds have not

yielded up the ghost until they were old as
Shem, Japhet, and Ham. An abandoned
cuckold, ostracizing himself because he had
become a ding-thrift for thirty to forty-five
minutes of calvish erotic sport with a doxy, no
more than a pin prick; and still understanding
Our Saviour's wisdom, 'The poor ye will always
have with you,' was marvelously content with
cloistral monkish penury. These cuckolds'
renegade wives, renouncing the canons of
wedlock prescribed by the Gospels, died senile
long before their husbands of a raging calenture
that also devoured ten to twelve paramours. Sir,
I've been mitred, goitered, horned, shorn; see, I
wear a nimbus, the ambiguous gift of fifty
shrews I met in seven to eleven bawdy houses. I
number my shame as a cabalist."

Father Moses, forgetting he was the
confessor and Christ's vicar, fell down to his
knees, mumbled through all the decades of
Aves, and groaned aloud: "Had I been the
disciple of the anchorite Don Pablo, subsisting
upon honey and locusts, I too might be in this
world long as Mizraim." About to kiss a latchet
fastened to one of Don Pablo's scruffy shoes, he
presumed once worn by James the Just, brother

of Jesus, for he had a marvelous veneration for relics, Father Moses recovering abruptly came to his clerical senses, but craving to restore his self-esteem as a priest furtively absolved himself of error.

Father Moses gently reprehended Don Pablo: "An excess of benefactions often is the show of the perverse pride of Nimrod."

Don Pablo: "All my sins are bitter aloes with which Jesus Christ was embalmed. Often was I fain to have my abominable flesh preserved with this Palestinian plant."

Father Moses, deeply impressed with Don Pablo's candor and self-abasement, said: "Should the Church fail to comfort your remains, God will provide the ram and the mummia. Are you still an acolyte of Paracelsus; then I must anoint you with a heifer's urine."

Don Pablo: "It is that peregrine Abel who tells me that the blood is salt and acid piss, and his cucurbit. Not I, Father, but Abel, the motley, should be punished by setting him in a cucking-stool solely for the jeers of sinless, pewed man."

Father Moses: "Would you acknowledge you're coarse?"

Don Pablo: "I am vulgar every hour; worse,
an unregenerate usurer who has lent money to a
widow. When she was unable to pay the
multiplied interest, I foreclosed her grove and
home. However, I never omit to greet an
impecunious workman since a warm salutation
is more essential to the spirit than bread."

"Infidel that you are, your mistakes are a
trifle, for St. Paul held that even the idolatrous
Greeks were pious." Father Moses' own mind
was meandering, and of a sudden he was not
certain where he had left off, or how to piece
together the confession. He placed his own
near-deceased hand upon Don Pablo's,
muttering, "My old child, humility must needs
be revered even in a disbeliever; for who can
gainsay that the meek shall inherit the earth?"
Abruptly he awakened from his own
slumbering divagations, vociferating to Don
Pablo: "I hear you've divorced eight wives and
inhumed as many concubines as Priam begat on
the body of Hecuba."

Don Pablo, likewise afar from the solemn
occasion, exclaimed: "A lie from the slanderous
tongue of Hag Slander who has the adder of
Medusa beneath her tongue. All I need to hear

is the word 'placenta' and I'm nauseous.
Likewise, I am closer to the winding sheet
when I smell the menstrous cloth."

Don Pablo, overthrown by his confessor,
begged him: "Forgive me, O Father Moses,
lest I have an everlasting quinsy in Hades."

"It is a redemptive wrong, not too late.
Should you ever be resurrected, be wary."

"I must disclose more," added Don Pablo.
"It has not been my goodness that prevented
me from committing sottish acts, but the fear of
being poxed by a Majorcan trollop. A damsel
who looked as lilied as the sepulcher, but as
roynish as a tart of Babylon within, endeavored
to seduce me in my primy eighties, claiming she
was the reincarnation of the hetaera, Thais. But
I sent her to a horrendous atheist, who
straightway received her incurable doctrine."

The priest was trying to chew his slipper
nose. Musing, he retorted, "I don't hold with
the Judaic testament. Be pure with the pure and
impure with the impure. Still, since you did not
get the botch of Egypt, your shameful parts are
not wholly at odds with Scripture. If, when you
were tempted, you gave alms to the Church and
tithing your anise and cumin did exulcerate

your conscience, I consider it a pardonable aberration."

Comforted by the priest's leniency, Don Pablo felt it necessary to exhume every imaginable foible in his decrepit bones. "Is there anything in mingling with a chit but a quartan ague one can catch without relinquishing one's religious principles?"

"Fornication, simony, rheumy gluttony, and adulterous Rahab radiant as Helen of Troy, are found everywhere in the Balearics." Father Moses lifted his brow, and exhorted Don Pablo: "You are indeed egregiously fleshy and heavy on your feet. When God gave you leave to walk and, alas, wander—were you at no time a gulch?"

"As a nervous boy, I had a puny palate. When I was seated over a bowl of soup, a harpy left a parcel of her bowels in it, and thereafter I ate with an indifferent appetite—were I a glutton I would have bitten a midge in my hors d'oeuvre really a caraway comfit."

Again, pondering the immense securities and bonds that Don Pablo held, he admonished him: "Can a man gain a fortune without sacking entire cities and sending thousands of

grievous workers to the cemetery long before
their time?"

More calmly, Father Rodriguez shook his
head with Catholic submission. "Only the
crop-sick utopian and diabolic Socialist believe
they can extirpate poverty and whoredom that
has sired many saints."

Easier in his mind, Don Pablo made another
disclosure: "Recently a succubus crept into my
bed at midnight and I grappled with her until I
yielded."

Father Moses: "Have you pilloried yourself,
my lad, for your visions of the night? What of
your marital concupiscence?"

"God forbid I should gender. Long ago I saw
how inane it was to have lawless lust for a wife.
I completely abstain from sexual commerce
with my spouse. Had I to commence once more
my ill-fated pilgrimage on this mizzling orb, for
it is a tear-bottle, I would be a celibate. At first,
marriage was a flux of foul and salt nights. The
words 'wife' and 'husband' are euphemistic
titles for lechery no man should utter lest he
contaminate Sagittarius and the galaxies of stars
in the canopied firmament. My wife was never
so trite as to call me husband, a fair enough

occupation for a fortnight. After that one
commences to think about carnal pleasure. No
different from a flea-bite, the drilling of a tooth,
or an itching scab. Such joys of the skin are
horrid as the gates of Hades. Administer my
last rites before my brain is a whirlpool of
madness."

"How long has it been, my well-timbered
boy, since you covered your spouse?"

"How can my pate, feeble as the cony, recall?
Besides, is not recollection whoremonging—for
what is there to remember except what is evil?
There's nothing to pleasure that's not in pain."

"How have you passed your recent days?"

"Really, I do not consider time to exist; for
what is the difference between one baleful week
and another?"

"That is an apocalyptic observation; for in
paradise there are no watches or clocks. Were
Gabriel and Michael to say to God, 'I'm busy,'
each would be cast into Hell. No man who
wears a wristwatch can ever drink of the living
waters of everlasting life." Pausing, the Padre
then asked, "Are you given to sloth, my
Catholic son?"

"All day long I think on Christ's sepulcher and my own."

Father Moses appeared to be fed by his lower lumpish lip and reflectively continued, "Adam was punished for supposing he was thinking. He, in hugger-mugger, snatched a leaf from the Tree of Knowledge of Good and Evil, and then insensibly began to age. For whenever a man supposes he has a thought he begins to die."

Father Moses continued: "Covering a woman is not so gross as human reason. Man will cleave to his faults more tenaciously than to a mother, father, or the Creator. Though God forbade man to eat of the Fruit of Good and Evil, that wombles in his mind and stomach, why is flesh so perverse as to partake of it. Soon as Adam pretended to be a thinker he decided he was logical. This so outraged God that he made Man the most unreasonable brute in the earth. He then confined him to the thistles and the briars, which are the office, factory, and aconited Sunday. Still infuriated with the rational beast he gave him countless ills, and to punish him more he built the spittle. Man's sole obsession is any crazy bauble. The meanwhile,

Adam toiling without profit to his soul on the
assembly line, did not concern himself with
Cain, who ran wild in the streets and stole for
pleasure, which the mundane Phillister has
coined 'commerce.' Cain also invented solitude,
the beginning of that new-fangled custom,
namely, to care for nobody.

"Tell me, my infant, have you ever been
reasonable?"

"Never, Reverend Father, although I
committed every other sin. Each time I
imagined I thought, I was thoughtless;
whenever I tried to be humble, I was
unbearable."

Father Moses: "Do you love your brother
more than Pleasure who sired Malice?"

"I exhort my brother continually and am no
better than the torpedo fish which loses all
feeling itself when it benumbs another."

Father Moses lowered his face and uttered,
"Are you addicted to epicurism?"

"After the manner of the stoics, I find one
olive a day sufficient, plus a pimiento to prevent
hardening of the arteries. My secondhand suits
and shirts I purchased half a century ago in
Kent at a frippery."

"Do you bear false witness against your enemies, particularly when they bite you?"

"I only bite myself since all my foes are within me. El Medico gave me a simple; that is, to boil a scorpion with wine, to guard against my charitable nature."

"You've been honest as flesh can be which lies and cogs. But there is a vipery doubt that stings my bosom. Have you divers bastards in different latitudes?"

"Unblemished Father, I am my only child."

Father Moses: "I cannot shrive you, my suckling, unless you divulge a tittle of your gargantuan bequests. Are you rich as Herod or covetous as Cleopatra?"

Don Pablo: "I wear my poverty on the threadbare elbows of my sleeves covered with carcase leather. What I am able to relate may sound like a clownish paternoster. Besides, how could I be a liar, when each night I wear my winding sheet, as a chaste widow who is covered with her mourning weeds.

"I admit my bequests are mean as Emperor Galha's avarice. Fifty thousand pounds sterling for a cloister and another 2,000 for a bawdy house to be metamorphosed into a priory;

4,000 for the portico of St. Bartolomé; 20,000
pesetas for twelve alms rooms at Fornaluxt to
be occupied by superannuated *obreros*. Also
5,000 pesetas for artichokes and lettuce to be
bestowed upon widows big with child. One
thousand pesetas for shoes of beef-witted
bastards; to dispend 15,000 pesetas for garlic,
Homer's Moly, to assuage a dispeopled ravine,
one kilometer from the Carthusian Monastery
on Valldemosa; and 300 pesetas for a Majorcan
boy or girl with a kilderkin of sense.

"I possess sardius, jasper, agate, and jacinth
emboweled in the Grecian Cyclades, to be
converted into tinsel wares, sundry specious
fabrics and criminal amusement boxes that clog
the heads of the rout and are a holocaust to all
nations in the earth."

Father Rodriguez wiped his eyes, and spoke
to Don Pablo as though he already were
wrapped in his shroud: "Let me admit that
you're now a shade; everything ebbs and dies;
only a sin is immortal. You have received
extreme unction; expire, my son, for man is
commonly dead every day anyway." The priest,
having finished, stood motionless and expectant.

Don Pablo was making ready to do what was

contrary to his merchant dogmas. On this
occasion he gave Father Moses a hundred
pesetas in addition to a hundred shares in the
Cunard Line. And, as a parcel of his reborn
faith in his brother, he pledged him fifty of his
swaddling clothes.

A mother's water welled up in the eyes of
Father Moses. As he was retiring, he bowed
thrice to Don Pablo, who, no longer able to
constrain his feelings, mumped his religious
fervor: "Sinner that I am, let me kiss your
angelic hand."

Father Moses, mewed up in his own holy
emotions, awakened from his revery, answered,
"I have wronged you, innocent suckling. No
man is quite what another person thinks he is."

Don Pablo thought Father Moses the most
guileless man he had ever encountered, and
Father Moses esteemed Don Pablo no less. But
less vigilant than a convert to Catholicism
should be, Don Pablo exclaimed: "I'd rather
have sage, onion, thyme, and parsley than the
four Gospels." By now Father Moses' ears were
as surd as his head; besides, he had
unexpectedly become a share-holder; so his sole
desire, awkwardly crooking his leg, as he

walked backwards, was to pick a thanks with benevolent Don Pablo.

For the balance of the day, people from the town called on Don Pablo to ask him whether he was dead. A notary public arrived promising to be his pallbearer without charging him a fee. Don Pablo's wrinkled, hidden eyes smiled; he had pledged the one hundred shares in Woolworth's to the notary.

Don Pablo had always believed he was void of the gross follies of an old dotard. He had viewed Genesis as a fable. Now he solemnly thought on it. Spite of the fact each hour hung by the thread of Ariadne he argued that Shem was a hundred years old when he begat Arphaxad, and dwelt among men for five hundred years. It was a consolation to consider that Peleg must have had Parkinson's disease, gall stones, kidney disease, and strangury when he was four hundred years old. Returning to Father Moses he pondered: Had he never thought he was thinking he could outface Methuselah.

Really, it was time he ceased thinking. He had long since concluded he knew a great deal of nothing. Let it be. He would die. Ah, he was

tired. Ninety-two caitiff years, all fallen angels.
What was the point of carrying on a brabble
with himself about the antiquity of Shem or
Mahalaleel or Canaan—all of whom had gone
into the ground? All this was bathos, the
pinchbeck flow of emotion.

PART II

It was noised abroad that a Virgin had come to No Hay Nada. The general gossip was that she had been hatched in a remote dunghill sandbar in the Celtic seas. Such news engendered a tumor of concupiscent sensations in the Majorcan. There was a hodgepodge of harebrained conjectures: An importer who frequently went to Cairo said a spotless dame was a Phoenicopterus, a water fowl from the river Nile, whose tongue was a morsel for any fleshmonger. He also opined a maidenhead could be *bitumen Judaicum* from the Dead Sea. Another stated there was no living female that did not have a chambered trait.

The villagers of No Hay Nada asked: "What

is a Virgin?" Was she a Naiad, goddess of the
wells of No Hay Nada, or the issue of foul
sewers, ditches, and highways where sylphs,
pigmies, giants, or a homunculus were sown? A
mad rustic, who rolled through the town on his
bicycle when the moon had grown its full
horns, told the elders, who had sapient noses
and the jowls of those who feed much but never
gender, that he had drawn up buckets of
maidenheads from his mother's well, which he
had made into a plaister of mosquitos, gnats,
and Afric flies.

The dispute continued: Chastity was a bezoar
or calculus in the matrix that routs the ugly
addendum, Priapus. Some dismissed virginity as
the kitchen-talk of servants.

The meanwhile it was reported that Don
Pablo was lying beneath the willows on the
banks of the famed river Styx. Others alleged
he was engaged to this newly arrived Virgin.
Lais O'Shea had a country pippin face, sandyx
hair, veins empurpled as seaweed near the
Pillars of Hercules, and the albic buttocks of
Aphrodite in a blackberry skirt.

Just then Doña Siegfrieda, spouse of Don
Pablo, passed the *circulo*. The old men lowered

their eyes. She had the galliard paps of the
Ephesian Diana, and her bobbed hair was
toothed as the serrated fins of the Barble fish.
She was wearing mourning weeds.

Sundry merchants appeared at Don Pablo's
Villa D'Or with hired weepers. The funeral was
set for the next day. The Proprietor of Colmado
la Luna was the first visitor. His emporium,
hard by the plaza, was filled with abstruse
comestibles: the barbecued anus of a
salamander, *paella* spiced with boiled frogs and
dressed with melted marcasites, and gneiss
adorned with kelp found at neap tide, roasted
toads, baked lizards piebald with a babe's
breath, coffee from the Antilles.

The Proprietor had a black band around his
sleeve. He was held in high repute because he
wore an occidental jacket and a cravat. He was
sure Don Pablo would join his ancestors in his
ninety-second year, and had advanced him fifty
thousand pesetas four days ago. In return Don
Pablo had told him that he would be the
beneficiary of a nursing home in Marbella
where unthrift dukes and counts had died
bequeathing the pox to their kindred. He was
also to receive three fabulous farms of lettuce,

celery, eggplants at Inca, the shoe town of the
Balearics, and a *finca* of melons at Maramar.

Wiping the electrum from his eyes, the
Proprietor could not govern his tongue hanging
from his mouth like the cuttlefish that casts its
gut to catch a sprat or sardine that might
imprudently come near enough to be pulled
into its craw.

Dolly Patch, brother to Don Pablo, whose
polemic nose always seemed to point either to
the northwest or to Pisces, caressed the
Proprietor's coat lapel, and moistened his
English cravat.

The Proprietor's words were laconic. "Is the
cerecloth here? And what hour will the Saint be
inhumed? Is this antique bay tree evergreen? Or
is his occupation dying?"

Dolly asserted: "I informed him that even
flesh of good worship is the same as ashes, dust,
mulch, that pester limbo. He's dead, but not
legally."

The Proprietor's visage, spurtled with wrath,
was about to glut his blood. "It's your fault.
You won't let him die."

"My holy brother is addicted to cavil; I have
advised him he would be more content with life

if he died." Dolly swore that only a half hour
earlier Pablo had dropped into his ultimate
frenzy, and had taken to bed a plaster of Paris
image of Mary Magdalene. He further
disclosed he had discovered hidden in the cellar,
beneath a pile of oranges and lemons, a basin
embossed with topaz and rubies in which Pilate
had washed his hands of the Truth.

"Pilate's Basin," whispered the Proprietor,
genuflecting, "is as sacred as Christ's
Sepulchre! Please include it in Don Pablo's
'petit testament' and 'grand testament.' " He
departed, giving Dolly Patch a *propina* of ten
pesetas.

The pious Margarita Concepción, usurer,
with an illegitimate, crookback hagseed and a
swollen gargoyle face, was catacombed in a
darksome room of her home.

In her shop she kept for sale gimcrack
images of Jesus, Mary, her mother Hannah,
and Joseph, as well as a gallimaufry of trumpery
relics, the embalmed leg of Ignatius of Loyola,
gegaw pictures of the little Christ in his crib,
and the Bible supposed to have been the exact
one St. Jerome held in his hands during his
divers orisons. She designed shrouds, engraved

funeral cards, furnished bereaved families with
photographs of their beloved kindred interred
in All Souls' Charnel. The store sat beneath
Puig Major. The most precious phial locked in
a showcase contained one stellar tear shed by
the Saviour on the Mount of Olives. When the
sacral vessel was removed and held up to the
light the tear was stained with gules red as a
ruby; on a gloomy day it shone like a pellucid
blue sapphire. Now every afternoon Señora
Margarita Concepción appeared at the Villa
D'Or carrying a hempen basket full of the
integuments of corpses to frighten Pablo who
looked empty as a cenotaph. She brought a
cerecloth of onyx, and one of garnet-red she
wrapped around his wide, hilly shoulders.
Quickly she displayed an albic winding sheet of
tafetta piebald with yellow hawkweed. Unable
to cheapen the burial sheet, Don Pablo viewed
the prehensile money-lending nose of the
ecclesiastical shopkeeper, and sent her away.
Four weeks earlier, in exchange of a loan of
100,000 pesetas at 300 percent monthly
interest, Don Pablo had given the
money-lender 50,000 shares in Sheffield steel.

    Then Don Bartolomé Avarioso arrived. His

triune bellies hanging beneath his deceased genitals shook seven cabalistical times with each step. Patch, observing him, said to himself, "By the ballocks of Hercules, his countenance resembles his gulligut haunches." Don Bartolomé was waiting for one of Patch's buracic quibbles.

Dolly: "During the night I felt his pulse thinly sighing as the Ephesian sod. Shaking, I bent over the larva, covered with pustules; here and there besides were buconic scabs and a canker. I was positive it had been bitten by a cockatrice. The spectre moaned without surcease. Hesitating, to weigh my love, I endeavored to trammel up my conscience, and forever abate the grief of the ghost by committing fratricide. Instead, I administered basilicon to the spewy imposthumes and resurrected the dead."

Don Bartolomé: "We know Don Pablo was an *amigo de falda* before he had departed this world; dead, wived, and betrothed are no violations of the Catholic doctrine of Trinity. But if now acting as a demonic outcast from heaven, claiming you've resurrected him, three will fall into one and the Church expire."

Dolly: "What I observed in a great amaze was the metamorphosis of a ghost. With infidel eyes I perceived that a disembodied phantom was translated into a mushroom spawn, then a moth blight, a liverwort, a Pythagorean kitchen kidney bean, a mosquito hawk. Filled with mortal superstitions, I ran down through the *huerta de abajo* and slept in a café chair until dawn."

Don Bartolomé cudgeled Dolly Patch's nose till it bled. "I suppose a ghost can also excrete."

Dolly: "Why not, it has nothing else to do."

Don Bartolomé tried to kick Dolly in the groin, but fell down on the patio, and Dolly helped him to his feet.

Don Bartolomé: "Liar, murderer of the doctors of Roman Faith, renegade Beelzebub! The Vatican, ever deciphering the unspoken stellar words of Archangel Gabriel, accepted without cavil Don Pablo's devout conversion of a Gentile and his total belief in the Holy Trinity. Nor did the Pope assume that a wayward child who had stepped into myriads of dotages would never mock Number 3, signifying the Father, the Son, and the Holy Ghost, by being dead, wived, and betrothed.

"Spite of the tender leniency of His Holiness, must you commit this sulphurous blaspheme! How could you act as an agent of a fiendish demon, tainted with hubris and impudicity whose sole purpose has been to skelder our church at Rome with an irreverent flout of the Triune Godhead so that 4 would be enthroned as Anti-Christ."

Don Bartolomé's wry contumely now lay on a wart tipped with twilight glimmering away: "When, pray, Devil Patch, do you expect the phantom to shed his divers marks?"

Dolly: "The lacerated phantasm has doubtless consummated all of his changes, and the corse now lies in the coffin."

Don Bartolomé: "Then he's irrevocably dead; otherwise he will harrow up all my nights flitting in and out of my idle-headed trances; either he's eluding the bumbailiff or befooling his naive and credulous beneficiaries. How can a Pythagorean kitchen kidney bean be buried in Holy Catholic ground? Should these hag-ridden visions be our sole bequest then we can anticipate an orphan purse."

Dolly: "Pity, Don Bartolomé, ever soft and mild as Christ's dusk. Think on the tribulation

of a Catholic wraith vexed unto death toiling for
his demise.

"Kindly dulcet devotee of our Saviour, wait
here; I'll visit the corpse indubitably lying
motionless as infinity in his bier."

Dolly issued from the darksome house, with
a rapt countenance. "Don Pablo was writhing,
struggling to get into his shroud, and irate
because it was too tight and pinched his paunch.
He swore his waistline was lean as a herring."

Don Bartolomé: "Is the apparition in a lady's
dressing room; does he mistake a cerecloth for a
bustle? Was he primping in front of a mirror
rubbing pomatum on his disembodied visage; or
is he fastening the laces of his stays?"

Dolly: "Dead or alive, people are implacably
the same. When he lived, he was froward,
caggy and contumacious. After attaining almost
a century of ugglesome years, he is a medley of
both sexes—now a sham man, then a bubbling
grass widow, a glut of hermaphrodite
crotchets."

Don Bartolomé: "Is this worm-eaten,
androgynous spectre, who's presently trying on
a corset, dead or alive?"

Dolly: " 'Tis an ontological enigma; he is and he isn't."

Don Bartolomé: "Are you implying the ghost is such a witling that he can't make up his mind whether he's a companion of the shades or alive?"

Dolly: "The subject is too tedious; no theologian I'm ill-prepared for an endless discourse of being and not being. Would not a digression becalm your fragile constitution?

"Recall Father Pablo's diction, pure as Parian marble, occasionally crumbled. He had a doleful lower colon that grieves his rhetoric that El Medico felt was the cause of aphasia.

"But never misdoubt his parental devotion to you. I distinctly remember looking over his shoulders whilst he cobbled up a mingle-mangle of codicils to favor you, and to cocker and summer your rusty, crapulent hopes. He larded your massy inheritance giving you entire ownership of a quarry of syenite near the First Cataract. The Pope sent a nuncio to *Abogado* Antonio Mentira, informing him the Vatican had forfeited its claim to the frankincense trees in Arabia Felix, originally Adam's. His

Holiness, appreciating Don Pablo's unwavering
fealty to the Rood, and likewise a paradigm to
schismatics, unfrocked scavengers of new
fangles and the debris of other sects."

Don Bartolomé's tumor of spleen ripened:
"What of the jointure promised the Virgin?
Not being a doctor of physic, is a maidenhead a
ringworm, a flux of pus, or just the fetid
perspiration of a bilious knap?"

Dolly: "You're an oracle, Blessed Bartolomé.
It's old maid's folklore, an obsolete word, a
pedantical reference in a drossy catalogue
known as *Home Doctor*, commonly hidden in
the buttery, behind jars of condiments and
crocks of electuary formerly used to remedy the
pox.

"In spite of your recondite learning you'll
expire of the apoplexy, for your egregious
concern about His Holiness, Don Pablo's
Gracious Will."

Dolly's mind began to meander supposing he
was Ceres searching for Persephone: "I suppose
maidenhead is a pathological term for a fungoid
excrescence, a parasitic membrane famed in the
reign of Thutmos II as the virgin jewel. Since
then archaeologists have been digging in

various parcels of countries, Burma, Yemen,
and Tartary, or excavating quartz, jade, gold,
heliotrope, but never locating a trace of this
gem more precious than the Philosopher's
Stone."

Don Bartolomé's pinguid head was nodding:
"Is this the kitchen-prate of a blowsy, ignorant
charwoman?"

Dolly: "This is more recondite than the
antiquary hieroglyphs of old Egypt's pylons. It
just occurred to me that El Medico thought this
obnoxious crevice (any cranny is likely to
awaken libidinous vagaries) could be stuffed
with half an ounce of henbane, two ounces of
scented oatmeal, steeped in syrup spiced with
monk's rhubarb, and thus hermetically seal the
vulva containing greater treasures than held by
all sovereigns everywhere. So, my brother close
to me as Don Pablo, be tranquil; why become
irascible, when you are a fragrant rumor of
benevolence, and the Antipodes of all snudges?
Henceforth, only men of autocratic intellection
will be privileged to inherit wealth." Don
Bartolomé swooned.

Dolly: "Excuse me, Knight Bartolomé, your
ecstasy has excited your armpits; they're

rammish. I'll fetch water from the well. Be so
noble as to remove your shirt and I'll throw
cold water over you."

Don Bartolomé: "True, we are solely
familiar with the wrinkled vestals of the church,
morphewed dwarfs who smell of the incense of
moles. Still, I'm sore perplexed since you
appear to hawk phantoms. Then bend your
mind on my quandary. This year I purchased
one gram of the sacred earth of Compostello for
his marmoreal urn. Within the past lustrum he
has had from me 7,000 citrus saplings, and
besides all that ordure, not a peseta in return."

Dolly: "As for excrement, Sir, we have no
need of it. Our Moor, Leandro, has diarrhea,
several furlongs of bowels, and discharges his
fundament enough to fertilize all Pablo's groves
and more than necessary to fill the jakes of
Cocytus."

Don Bartolomé's doubting malmsey nose
was now almost sanguinary in color: "I fear I'm
being flead; I smell a gangrened quibble."

Dolly: "How can I allay your vermiculate
skepticism? Who can fathom the preter-human
faculties of Saint Pablo, not those of the human
race or the sleepy, indotent Lotopagi?

"Did I not hear in your presence His Grace
say 'Gramercy, Don Bartolomé Avarioso, for all
your ordure.'?

"Several days ago just before the chimes of
even-song, El Medico mentioned a pottle of
vermifuge drugs so potent it could expel every
uterus in the Balearic Isles."

Don Bartolomé: "Very reassuring, Señor
Patch, were it not for that other swindle, the
teats, popinjays, and riggish lubbers deem
exquisite kickshaws triturated with sugar. This
school of goatish rogues claim they bruise and
crush the nipples as an apothecary pulverizes
the bark of a red Peruvian tree."

Dolly: "Spite of his bedellium, the diamonds,
the celanese farms of pepper, and the mangrove
trees in the Antilles, Sage Pablo, knowing that
Fortune is with Heaven and that his malignant
half-faced brother Poverty may, on a sudden,
craftily suck up your lands, houses, barns,
farms, orchards, goats, amended his Testament
to spare you.

"Therefore, Lord Pablo provided you with a
fictile vase gorged with dried roots of water
trefoils, a sextary of meal to knead and bake the

bread of lamentation should sly Penury entrap you."

Don Bartolomé: "I suspect may be a shake-rag wandering the earth in an outworn drugget."

Don Bartolomé going away and shambling along past the well and through the arbor wept aloud: "O my dung, adorate as jasmine and precious as jacinth; now all this costlew ordure is in Don Pablo's orchards."

Don Bartolomé's swag-bellied gait was sluggish as he wailed aloud: "Don Pablo has stolen all my dung." *Abogado* Don Antonio Mentira arrived and said, "Who now has meddled with his last farewell and fiftieth will?"

Dolly asserted, "Don Antonio, his ultimate testament is as void of spot as our Blessed Lady. But since you drew his bequest two days ago, his Honor, Don Miguel Gomez Menos O Mas, the notary public, has increased your properties. Think on it, you'll inherit an Elysian brothel filled with adust hetaerae and milky skinned slaves brought over by Cristóbol Colón from the Antilles on his second voyage."

The *Abogado*: "Am I to lie with maggots as my paramours and lemans?"

Dolly: "My cherished friend, every beauty will shortly be a worm, and a cuckold should always bear that in mind."

The *Abogado*: "Never mind your crafty dissimulation."

"Sweet Antonio Mentira, I am referring to their saffron descendants. I take my buskined oath on three bibles—our divine Catholic, the heathen Koran, and the Judaic Scripture of those stiff-necked Pharisees, scribes of the Old Testament—that he regards you as his son. Now your patrimony will be myriads of leagues of myrrh, ivory from Sudan, ebony and jade from Tartary."

The *Abogado*: "Perjuries! Don Pablo has a granitic heart. The entire human race has set the example for him by dying. But he won't do it."

Dolly: "My minion, Antonio, you will also receive seven tea farms in India with two hundred Moslem mamelukes you can constuprate. My worshipful brother has not a dram of unkindness in his bones all filled with moldy disappointments. However, he has set aside 100,000 pesetas for an almshouse in Fornaluxt which will contain fifty beds with

pillows stuffed with the plumage of the eider
that frequent the estuaries of the frozen poles.
Think on it! Do you really believe a savant is
such a simpleton as to wish to repeat his life and
be a fool twice? I grant your name has not been
on his sacral lips, but a near cadaver has a great
deal of numb feelings for nobody."

Don Antonio scratched his skinny oleaginous
nose, his five hairs flying about like a noisome
starling, and spoke: "Grouthead, why do you
geld my expectations?"

Dolly: "Never, sir, for I have more canorous
words for your ears. He has likewise
bequeathed to you three diamond mines in the
suburbs of Cape Town."

Antonio flared, "May you gulp down your
mildewed falsehoods and expire writhing in a
spittle."

Dolly: "Be comforted, please! He's sick of
the mulligrubs, and his thin, pinchbeck life
hangs downwards toward Styx."

What's this noise about a Virgin from the
Antipodes? Is a maidenhead a study in first
causes? Does it not require St. Thomas of
Aquinas to interpret a vestal, for nature, and its
putrid spawn, skin, is maculate?"

As he left, he was mumping his misdoubt:
"There are more gimcrack codicils in his
testament than hairs on Abraham's head."

El Medico Muchas Pesetas stepped on the
patio reading passages of Hippocrates, until
involuntarily raising his globular cranium to set
eyes on pygmaen Dolly; a sudden tidal fury
took hold of him. "I've given the sainted Don
Pablo the essence of a viper daubed with the
saliva of Judas, seven ounces of black hellebore,
and he gained three stone. Do you know how
much of his legacy he has made over to this
putative Virgin?"

Dolly blurted, "Go soft! Fifteen minutes
before your arrival he pleaded with me to let
him die; there was a ring of burning boils
circling his feverish brows; and he complained
of a splay-footed Gorgon who skulks to his bed
by midnight and spoils his knees of all their
radiant noon. Kind brother that I am, I hung
leeks and figs over his doorway to expel another
evil that might burden him."

El Medico: "I prescribe dried grapes and sod
pine cones to abate Don Pablo's papaverous
condition. On the morrow, go to the apothecary

for Ramnos Tristus and the resin of the fir tree
which might expurge his madness. Dry lunacy
is not so noxious and protean as moist
hypochondria under the spell of watery
Aquarius. He wishes to die, but at the
penultimate moment he alters his mind. I've
pronounced him dead eight times. How baffling
it is to understand why anybody should cling to
such a disease as life which even I can't cure.
Now the gravediggers smirk when I go to the
cemetery to make sure my patients have the
quiet to which they are entitled."

"Sir, what can you suggest to melt my
brother's spleen?"

El Medico: "He should eschew dew lest a
damp fall into his liver, the seat of affections,
and he consequently be the captive of
melancholia. Have him inhale desert air and the
driest branch of a Joshua tree at 130 degrees of
solar rays."

"His face is a botch of Egypt."

El Medico: "Or we might experiment with a
contrary conceit; take him to San Sebastian, or
some northern parcel of Iberia where the
laurels will nourish and give him sufficient
strength to expire, this vestal or jill will be his

Dog Star and parch his infinite largesse but
restore his strength."

El Medico's tumid, rubbery face fell.
"Señora Felicia Gonzales, who owns the
lecheria has shut her shop, alleging that a
maidenhead has infected her eggs, honey, and
butter, and is as baleful to her milk as thunder,
a troop of ants, or the hieroglyphic prints of
mice on her cheese."

Dolly: "Don Pablo has his venal suspicions.
Not yet canonized, he's still bone, blood, flesh,
and excrement. But be assured no wren guards
the crocodile from his mortal foe, the
ichneumon, Pharaoh's Rat, with less vigilance
than he protects the bequest belonging to you."

El Medico: "Be plain, are you implying that
his Most Pious Reverence has again declined to
be united with his carrion kindred?"

Dolly: "Alive he's a snudge to you; once
dead, you'll be startled by his spiced conscience.
The Old One looks for posthumous
appreciation. Prince Pablo is a true Catholic,
and knows that a Spaniard values two teeth of
St. Martin more than a kind act. He told me
yesterday that you will receive an immense
forest of cork trees in the outskirts of Cadiz.

And as a further warranty of your impregnable virtues, he has left you a gallipot of barley water."

El Medico: "This is patchery! Are you suggesting that I, a regal descendant of Hippocrates and Galen, require a quacksalver of medicine to advise me to take a diuretic for my kidneys that have never troubled me?"

Dolly: "I beseech you, proffer a carease dotard a drachma of grace."

Dolly: "Is not Doña Siegfrieda ready to cocker his whimsies? For despite the constellations of his intellect, who's older than an old fool? He's fallen into a dotage over a drab whose tresses are odoriferous as caraway. May every trollop be devoured in her roynish fires. Loving brothers, all I can do is helplessly observe Don Pablo wantoning in the ashes of the clean-swept mind of a lotus eater. Repeatedly I've warned him he's ninety-two, and that the space between us in years is as vasty as the undecipherable kosmos."

El Medico muttered, "I am uneasy, Señor Patch. I suspect that what I will receive from him are cantharides, and I can pass water without them."

When El Medico had vanished, Dolly mused upon the bizarre erotic exhilaration of men. Though his brother was a libertine, he felt every time he took a spouse to bed Don Pablo regarded it as an assignation. No matter how Pablo attempted to dulcify his perverse imaginings, he was certain his wife or paramour was a trollop. It is custom for all chambering females to assume a modest carriage. Besides, virtue in a woman is plagiarism. O what a yoke of misfortune is a spermal man.

The meanwhile, Mercedes, the *criada* who did nothing but never ceased doing it, crept into Don Pablo's bed and began nuzzling at his dug. With one vascular elbow, he flung her to the floor, where she sat whimpering.

Abel was on Calle la Luna. The sky was a bony, bleeding Christ; and one could see a rib of granite above the two-storey houses. A short while ago he had taken a pound of tobacco, a snippet of sweaty bodice, a small cup of *vino corriente,* and brayed them with a pestle in a mortar and after drinking this beverage expected to be less of a witling with Dolly Patch. Presently he slubbered over his decision to walk to the Villa D'Or. Then he went back to Calle Manzana, a dirt road that ended in wild olive trees.

Issuing from the grove, he was once more on Calle la Luna, and of a sudden joy rimmed his eyelids. There was El Medico Muchas Pesetas coming towards him. What a man of feeling to an unfriended urchin in the winds! Abel stumbled against him.

"What is your most bizarre ailment today, Señor Abel? Imbibe bragget, eight aspirins with the draff of your hapless evenings."

"El Medico, I swallow twelve pellets before midday. Still three of my five intellectual fingers on my right hand are moldy, and the other two are in a spittle. When kites fly it is a sign of clear, dry weather; however, by nightfall the chill of bad news settles in my stygian knees, and I know I am coming down with a fit of misluck."

"Have you never enjoyed coition? Never lie with a wench in a room facing *Puig Major*. A swift watercourse could be beneficial. Be continent when the *torrente* is dry, or if you have the vapors. Rid yourself of any occasional spell of venery by lying half an hour each day in St. Faith's metal bedstead."

Abel's head was deaf. Was El Medico a whoremaster? Abel, for no cause whatsoever, viewing reason as a renegade to natural feeling, chanted: "When it's humid in Palma and the catarrhal grubs dote on the persimmon, the sun is in the almond trees of No Hay Nada."

Abel without knowing it grasped El Medico's gulligut trousers. El Medico grew choleric. "Insolent *hombre,* do you dare lay a finger on me? I'm not your almoner or a mountebank for lunatics afflicted with lepry human affections. You have disregarded my sovereign prescription. Perhaps you suppose you can reject my counsel by fobbing. Have you been stricken with that mortal disease called delay?"

"No, sir. I make my errors right away. When I wait to do something wrong my face is decorated with sores that resemble the bloodworm."

El Medico: "If water masters fire in the soul, the consequence is humid imbecility. Doubtless your ill is a colic; remember this simple: seeds of sea lavender mingled with malmsey physic a herringbone jacket that repulses the spider. Should you visit the remains of Thebes its

famous ruins should dilate your arteries. A
sojourn at the mound of Borsippa could
postpone glaucoma, or stay dysentery by taking
Mekon Kerratites after each meal."

Abel: "Please, El Medico, I drown your pills
with the jubilation of Neptune who bolts down
his foamy craw any Nereid he happens to see."

"I've had a heavy, bilious morning, and now
you gall me. I, too, must scamble up some
composure."

"I beg you, life is composed of timber of the
gallows. May I be truthful, which I allow is in
bad taste?"

"Go chew acorns and masts. Don't bother
me. What do you know of the Virgin?"

"Only what I've heard, sir. I've seen her
thrice. Each time she has a new mien; I wonder
if she is a hydra beneath a plane tree." Abel
rambled on: "A hawk mewed up in a cage came
in the mail last Wednesday; I inspected its
entrails, though I'm no spagyric."

By now Abel had separated El Medico from
his jacket; the latter paid no attention to Abel's
frenzy. El Medico was on his way to the town
hall, only about twenty meters' distant from

Abel who was standing as though that were a
vocation.

Then Abel followed him hard by his heels,
still murmuring, "Excuse me, is not such an
expression as 'Pardon me' as fragrant as the
desert tamarisk? It's a riffraff age of shame
kenneled like any mongrel. The mothers give
the milk of their sere teats to the gray-haired
sons until they are fifty years old. The rabble
have toy minds and the latest bauble drives
them mad. This dusk I'll take fourteen aspirins
to heal my small wheaten understanding."
Nobody heard him, but who does?

El Medico's sole purpose was to leave Abel's
hurly-burly behind him. He was attempting to
enter a revolving door, but he was buffeted into
a fury. Then two prudish faggots, in
kitchen-midden, house-dresses, came out. They
stepped on his feet. When El Medico cried out,
they blew the noisome breath of a chimera in
his face and hurried away. The door kept
rotating, and his hand was bruised as he
endeavored to capture one of the doors. "Our
Lord, divine Mary and Joseph, does one have to
be an engineer to enter a building?" But he

managed to take into the grip of his virile hand one door composed of kale, viperine mushrooms, and deceased funeral flowers. He then tore one door into pieces, and went into the civic hall.

Meantime, Abel went back to his rock-ribbed hovel, and tossing to and fro in his bed like restless Lucifer, he saw in the night a marish shadow with a knob in the middle of its forehead, standing at the foot of his bed. The spectre struck his head until it sank into his neck. Before vanishing it mocked him because he had raised a ghost he supposed was life.

In the morning after his trance, overwhelmed with coward forebodings, he cut a fresh branch of a plane tree, plus fleawort, and seethed them in a limbeck. He did this to medicine his poltroon premonitions of a yoke of another day. Was he afraid that he might fall in the dust after a quip from the froppish mouth of Dolly Patch; who can be clever with a dullard? Patch was no ninny, and spite of Abel's pleasantness, he was never able to dulcify his hard-headed contumely. Alas, all of Abel's retorts issued from his mouth a month later.

Any hour was a hanging of his disposition at
Old Bailey.

Abel rebuked himself for his fretful presage.
Who knows what can happen a half hour
hence? By then he was at the root of Calle la
Luna.

An *obrero* in filthy, tattered denim drawers, a
shirt that gives off the odor of stale spinach, and
wearing *alpargatas*, hempen cloth and rope tied
about his naked ankles with strings, stepped out
of the public latrine. He was scrathing his
groin, whilst a crumpled old damsel of the
church was picking her nose. The No Hay
Nadans did not deem an agynary vestal of the
church a female. None ever supposed that she
had ever had the odorate maidenhead.

The whole hamlet smelled of the menstruous
cloth. Hard by the jakes was St. Teresa's pump.
It contained a pair of metallic eyes through
which poured the tears of the sacral Jewess.
Abel passed a recess in a granite wall inside of
which was a gory Christ illuminated by a beige
electric bulb. He loitered, recalling his
peregrination from the French frontier to
Pamplona; the hips of the dank mountains were

covered with gorse and heather that steamed
like cat's piss.

Just then, a padre smelling of camomile
seated on a motorcycle, and attired in a crisp,
black, fluxional cassock, was flying to the
Mount of Olives. The vehicle upon which he
was mounted was called "Vespers,"
manufactured by the daughter of the deified
Generalissimo who had slain two million
Spaniards in order to keep the machine of the
Western World out of medieval Iberia.

Abel regarded the vanishing cleric: "Christ's
Vicar is void of all trumpery, for he never goes
barefoot or walks half a kilometer to bless the
orchards or to asperge the lewd nuptial
chamber."

Don Bartolomé paused to salute Doña
Siegfrieda, and asked with pious cant how her
sainted husband fared.

Doña Siegfrieda kept poultry, but such was
her chastity that there was no cockerel in the
yard to tread the hens.

Don Bartolomé bent over his several
paunches to kiss her hand. "Doña, don't grave
your stellar beauty. Remember the widow,
Señora Porphyria Robert y Mal, who died at

the age of one hundred twenty-seven, and
would still be seated in the garden observing
the *nisperos* hanging from the branches, had she
not eaten one hundred twenty-five *gambas* in
one evening."

Abel passed them with a hurried nod since he
regarded every human encounter a fatal musket
shot. The meanwhile he was on his way to
Biniaraix, and stopped to admire a Moorish
patio clustered with cyclopean pots of
aspidistras, geraniums, rhododendrons, aloes,
and cacti. A *criada*, with her slovenly cotton
dress tucked up above her drawers, was
scrubbing the stone floor. She turned to babble
with another servant in Mallorquin, a
corruption of Catalan, Arabic, Spanish,
Portuguese, Italian, French, that sounds like a
man blowing his nose. The roosters in No Hay
Nada crow at all hours, commonly at dusk.
Momentarily, Abel considered The Word that
became flesh, and perplexed by an anti-epical
century, exhorted the pestilent age of
foster-mother jargon: "This is the Last Supper
of the Logos; would that I had the tongue for a
phillipic against our unhouseled
alley-language."

The terrain was a Job's dry sherd, though
the February almonds were beginning to pink.
For him, February was the month of hearses
and grubs, cypress, gnashing of teeth, and
cracking bones beneath apish tombs. Not
realizing that a few No Hay Nadans were
watching him with avid pleasure, Abel cried
aloud: "I know the Alpha and Omega of
solitude. Loneliness is a wild dying. Wherever I
dwell I'm in the forest of Nõdh. Every man
who is Abel is also Cain, for there is nothing
good in man that is not bad."

Abel gazed at the teleological mountains of
sandstone, lime, feldspar, and conglomerate
venerable rocks of headstones, and godhead. He
fell into a dotage on gneiss, quartz, silver,
carbuncle and the Andes. He returned again to
Calle Manzana and walked into the grove of
olives, to sit beneath the oracular wood of
Minerva and hide from the world, a perpetual
throbbing anguish that had no visible use
except to ulcer his nerves. "Still," Abel
thought, "the falsehoods of Dolly Patch should
not shake or dupe me, for when a man lies he is
telling the truth about himself. Do I not feed on

putrid dreams and my ruins? Would that
willow, elm, maple, the acorns of Circe mixed
with the poisonous grimace of a Medusa might
be an antidote to my rueful noons, middays, and
aguish fears of sleep that cankers the morrow.
Why is it I always am ill-prepared for any
experience?"

Abel knew that Don Pablo was deceased,
wived, and about to be engaged to the Celtic
jillflirt, Lais O'Shea. Before he assumed he
could risk wearing the fool's coat in the
presence of Dolly Patch, Abel gulped down
several drops of Muria, dragon's blood, a haw,
and recited a few parables, and soon he arrived
at the Villa D'Or.

Dolly: "You live by yourself. Isn't that
tiresome company, Abel? I hear you're pluming
your quasierudition and putting on airs with the
villagers. Why are you so ill-natured, always
carping of my rare temperament?"

Abel: "Señor Patch, I have no such abilities
in polemics; I would be out of my mind could I
imagine I were your superior in the flowerless
subtleties of argument, in that I could presume
I were a peacock of learning in your divine

presence. I am so naturally humble that I doff my hat to the worms that inevitably will, after I'm dead, tickle me to death."

Abel opened his eyes and saw Lais O'Shea seated with her knees hermetically sealed together. She rose, curtsied to him, sat down, and remained an obelisk of silence.

Don Pablo was in his curule chair. His broad, inky nostrils inhaled the storax of Lais's underclothing. Don Pablo reprehended Dolly as he spoke: "Abel, there's nobody; we suppose there's someone. We're spectres, and shortly disappear with the setting Pleiades. Death is a mild Doric word for the Maggot. Nature always has been a stepmother to human flesh; she furnishes it with vicious nights and when the bones are graved, their shades shriek: 'What is more of a horrendous mirror of our life than our dreams, direful forebodings of the everlasting anguish of the flagitious bones. Oh, could I have vanquished Lust, Death would be peace, not agony.'"

Dolly: "Are you saying that a corpse has visions?"

Don Pablo: "Born to die, though our lives are short, the days so tedious and prolix that we

pine away because we cannot wait for another
day; we cobble up our hours, impatient for
another twenty-four hours of monody. Abel,
what do you think?"

Abel: "Sir, I don't think."

Don Pablo: "That's a remarkable
observation."

Dolly: "Brother, you're an indefatigable
rationalist."

Don Pablo: "Reason, what is it but pedantic
trash, the sire of spite and the academic
dumps."

Dolly: "You're a logician, tell me why is
your nose in the middle of your face?"

Don Pablo: "Abel, don't lean on me like a
limpet to a rock; my blood's too thin and true
for affection. I have never been a friend to
myself or to anybody else. He who acquires a
friend demands to be harmed, bankrupted, and
an outcast."

Abel: "I'm ready to drop a warm, liquid tear
for anyone who eats bread. Later, I'm
humiliated for doing it. I feel especially dirty
after I've helped somebody."

Lais went into the house, returned with a rug
which she wrapped around Pablo, knelt, and

kissed his Jovian knees, and then quietly left.

Dolly turned to Pablo: "I hear that lungers, paralytics, costermongers, crookback dwarfs gratify her. Ruttish Venus joys in moles, a polt foot stench of the teeth, a running sore. She has the pinions of a fowl, and the intellect of a spider. She never talks which would be kind were she not always silent. She's mummified stupidity.

"How is it a man of ninety-two hasn't learned enough to recognize that the uterine tribe is spiteful, salacious, and ever ready to cuckold a clodpole miscalled a husband. Your nuptials will be a draught of hemlock. Infantine guilelessness may expect her to remove her placket, but the malkin will shower you with buttery—while fobbing you until you, ageless Cronus, snore like a spring tide.

"Your marriage will be a pleurisy of upbraids and adulteries with fishmongers, who use doggery to enjoy fornication the more, porters of latrines, a drayman, a scullion, a waiter, a poulterer stinking of the scalding house.

"I met a she at the hedge tavern, a maltworm wearing high-toned lockram who mentioned

Lais O'Shea with some misprision. I agree, she would as lief break a bottle of *Carlos Pirmera* as tell a truth.

"There was another she I ran into at the *bodega* who latched her tongue onto my waistcoat. Both were astonished how Lady Lais did tipple, and when a worker entered how she fixed upon him her glazed eyes, sunk in her veined skin of a bluish white deepened with antimony, as if she could drink up the whole man.

"Of course, they were a pair of strumpet liars; but just turn a she-lie about in the sun, and the truth will shine in your eyes. Is there an electuary for Lais' falsehoods?"

Don Pablo: "People who tell lies are more cozy and congenial than rock-hewn truth-sayers. The soft, dove-brained female tribe is addicted to perversity. An honest woman is false to the entire female race. How is it that a fat-brained boy of eighty-six doesn't understand that man was born to be the dupe of women? Let it be; we're all vassals of skirts, the Southern Cross, the Frozen Zone, and the Milky Way.

"Oh, I have swallowed myriads of shrunken

lakes, the scum of deceased ponds, a well-nigh treeless firth, violet meadow mornings at prime noon, and cast out pickthank friends with gutwort.

"The greater part of your misogamy is venal; the other cause of your invective humbug is that you're a muggish homuncle who couldn't raise a flickering ember in a vagabond-laced mutton."

Dolly: "I'll inscribe on my headstone: 'Here lies straight, rude Ingratitude, who was never a meacock beggar.' "

Don Pablo: "Wild ass of Edom, you've snuffed up my exchequer as though it were the fragrant wormwood tree."

Dolly: "You furnish me with what's left in the tins of sardines, Majorcan bread tough as the bole, and half a pint of two-peseta *vino corriente*. You've even told me to eat my hunger. Woe is me, I'll leave this world penniless."

Don Pablo: "Witling, once out of this world what need have you of a farthing?"

Don Pablo, turning to Abel: "There's a whirlwind of madness in my doomsday heart, with no tamarisk to umbrella it. But let that

beef-witted brother cease his glut of black bile
so that I can relish Lais's sapid petticoats. I
know I'm decayed, and old men smell; do I
stink like King Asa's feet?" A tear fell upon his
mummy-skin, for Pablo had not wept since
Abraham slept beneath the terebinth tree.

Don Pablo: "I fear myself because I'm
costive. An old, costive man is no better than a
privy. Why are the meager hours left me too
heavy even for Atlas to hold on his back?"

El Medico came for a moment, took Don
Pablo's pulse, and said he would tell the
undertaker to wrap his remains in mullein
leaves just as figs are clothed so that they won't
give off an evil odor. Then El Medico hurried
away, and Don Antonio Mentira arrived, who,
failing to perceive Don Pablo, announced to
Dolly: "If he's not yet dead, he is cony-catching
the entire town. He's more antique than Joppa
that existed two years before the Flood."

Dolly, drugged with satiety because he was
ignored, cried out: "Unlike Janus's door, Lais is
never shut. She has a most hospitable vulva.
Take care, lest she be infected as the woman of
the Moabites. She's a callet; have you the
carrion appetite for rust, the scum of lichens,

and the slime of a rotting creek? She's the water closet deity of love, Astarte, the fornicatress. If you stink, you're her paramour. A wheel because it rolls might also arouse her. Though not wed, she's already provided Pablo with the bitter aloes of cuckoldry. Does he suppose he can cinder Ilium for a slattern? 'Tis a pity for a man to handle a woman whilst he himself is a numb statue. Does Nestor expect to be a swift copulating on the wing?

High dawn he had the scall of Judas at the Last Supper. I touched his feet and they were cold and dank as Styx. He sleeps most of his crabbish day, shackled with rank snores, only opening a gummy eye to rail on me to leaven his spurious esteem. I know my brother abhors me, but I'm his fifth wall."

Don Pablo: "Muzzle the mushroom tongue of a eunuch boy of eighty-six. Suppose you're right about Lais; am I to thank you for depriving me? Besides, I hate a liar, especially when he tells the truth."

When Don Antonio saw Don Pablo, he left apace.

Abel: "Don Pablo, I am always in the Guinea Calms. I do nothing because I am afraid of myself. Should I call a man good he's sure to be bad, or say it's a fine day it's likely to be a worse one. I guess I have a hackneyed soul."

Don Pablo: "Abel, you're no fop who has washed all the calvish lines from his face."

Dolly: "There's a mark of cant in Abel's carriage; he walks about as if he were the town crier of Holy Writ. Observe my frigid continence. Even were I Saint Laurence, not a stale could roast me upon her whorish gridiron."

Dolly would not desist: "One must credit my brother's bones, he can smell his way to a sloven several kilometers before she passes through the arbor, goes by the well, and presents herself to him on the patio. This saint can weigh her fundament in the Scale of Themis, as well as her underclothes of Egyptian flax, or the goffered silk of the mulberry. The elders at the *circulo* claim they've seen the Virgin beat the Plaza Bartolomé, and say she lowered her coy eyes, gazing solely upon the cobblestones ornamented with offals, and her cheeks were wimpled modestly to mask the brothel virtue of a *dama de la media.* Such a trull is no different from Agrippina who likewise veiled her lechery. At Villa D'Or, she won't even cross her legs. You'd imagine she were a psalm of virtue. No sage can outwit a milkfed chit's miching malicho. Who comprehends the Spanish proverb so well as he: 'El Diablo viejo sabe mucho.' "

Dolly continued: "I'm poorer than any pismire, or a carpet everybody treads upon without pity. I coveted the surfeit of your vast graith, countless groves of orange, lemon, and grapefruit trees, diamond mines in Rhodesia, your large and heavy carracks plying the seas from Cape Town to the Azores, the garners in the Midi, entire streets filled with edifices and parrots of Segovia, and all the precious metals cited in the Book of Psalms.

"Each night I lay on the thin, feeble pallet, worse than a bed in a lazaretto, lent to me by my almoner, His Grace, Don Pablo. I coughed, enough to kiln all my skin, and I was sure I had a sweating sickness or a canker in my left ear. El Medico prescribed twenty aspirins a day for my urine and suggested he remove my gallstones and carve my neck and shoulder. El Medico's flummery pellets are fashioned in a smithy on Vulcan's anvil."

Don Pablo, weary of his barbs, said: "Bite
your fatuous prate. I fear a weanling. The seven
lean kine in the river Nile will always eat up the
seven rank fat heifers. O Hobbinoll, you're not
one fool, you're all of them. Do you suppose
you could endure good fortune which, as Pindar
says, is one of the daughters of Ocean?"

Don Pablo gave his attention to Abel: "You
have such a humble mien; but the honey is in
the carcass of the lion."

Abel: "I don't believe in life and life is not
particularly interested in me. That may account
for my meek countenance. I have no choice but
I seem to make it. Then, doesn't each person
covet his own defects, rather than somebody
else's? Everybody is simply the prey of his own
nature. Each one cleaves to his vices. Although
there's no free will, only a scullion will behave
as if he had no choice. All of a man's mistakes
belong solely to him. One foible begets another
just as Abraham bore Isaac, and Isaac, Jacob.
That's why advice is useless."

Dolly interfered: "Abel Bedlamite! Don't
you understand that Lais's skirts, with spots of
calcedony, sapphire, and ruby, are the flags of
adultery? She's a museless meretrix bred up on

Irish turf, rain, and mire; yet her stays,
chemise, and petticoats have far more influence
upon man than Aristotle's *Ethics*."

The mention of Lais stirred some coals of
jealousy in Pablo's blood. "Alas, this perfumed
heath has come to me only with the fall of the
leaf. Abel Aesculapius, physic me with Aurus
Potable."

Abel: "Sir, I am the helpless prey of a very
dangerous adversary, myself. Lately, El Medico
prescribed two granules of twilight mingled
with Poseidon's salt and the blood of a
maidenhead imported from Libya so I could
master at least one of my five senses. It could be
a simple for your own quandary."

Dolly declaimed, "That *mala bolga*, Lais,
cannot even spell pox."

Don Pablo: "Too many precepts in a woman
are likely to calcine her womb."

Of a sudden Doña Siegfrieda came, her eyes
wet—"Am I a widow?"—and went into the
house.

Dolly: "Is pleasure worth the pain one pays
for it? There's never been a bed that was not
dry as chaff for you after a fortnight. A
tottered, tombed Nestor, a mound of rubble

formerly sandy Sparta, still presumes he may
toy with a pigeon. So Doña Siegfrieda's potent
thighs no longer console you? Better a dry,
cropless bed than to be cuckold in a foul,
lubricious boudoir. Sometimes I think your
nose is all the intellect you possess. O wineless
blood and bones, where are your paramours?
All your courtesans, like dead acacias and
sycamores, lie in different countries beneath an
obscure heap of earth, or are under a tumulus
that once was Egypt's Apu famed for its linen.
Do you not worship any body, divine or
heathen, except Saint Scratch, Saint Rub, and
Father Lucre? Or lickpenny that you are, why
did you spend your force and pound sterling
upon that Elizabethan punk from York for
lodging, slippers, lavish suppers, and pomatum,
while my food was a trencher filled with
penury? Observe the crank, leaky wrinkles in
your visage which buffoon merchants in No
Hay Nada mistake for suffering crucifixes.

Don Pablo: "You were dry, wizened, and
abstemious in all equinoxes. You paint spleen
with umber that has as many colors as the
moth. Your rancor wambles in my gullet.
Compare me, if you like, to a Moabite

cromlech, or to a cairn where Abraham saw
Jehovah. Yes, I'm old, and age each time you
utter a platitude."

Don Pablo: "I abhor the fleers upon the face
of a Sunday pew-Tartuffe. Flout a lecher who
seeks a damsel whose eyes are a fountain of
angelic water for my wild Beersheba. The body
always has been my oracle; when I used my
head what I did was no better than the vermin
doggerel of the priestess at Delphi.

"Lais's past belongs to her. Whether she be
the maidenhead of my last days, or a brachette
baked and broiled in flamy whoredom, let her
be redeemed in my dissolute, but penitent,
flame."

Dolly Patch: "I confess a doxy is two
syllables too many for me; but I expect to
mature when the sun enters the sign of the
Ram."

Don Pablo: "When the bitter snows of the
Poles and a flamy chimera, and Jupiter sheds its
gore, and the dead carry their tombs abroad,
call yourself mature. Human flesh is too feeble
to understand itself. Seldom it is for people to
act sensibly since commonly they waylay in
dudgeon friend or enemy."

Dolly Patch: "Regardless of your glorious wisdom, I intend to be the pensive troglodyte requiring nobody except myself."

Don Pablo: "We are solitary alive and alone in our graves; that is Nature's fell purpose."

Dolly Patch: "You're very devious about everything and suggest that as I am your galliard brother I should be courteous enough to enter the steamy sulphur waters of hell before you. Does one have to be that polite for a near kin? Relic, you've consummated your scrannel Iliad on this earth, and senseless stock, you won't admit it's ended. May Jupiter praise monarch Venom. I abhor anybody who feigns he's good, who's only good-for-nothing."

Don Pablo's back was smoldering, but he maintained a mute head, insisting that "Lais was odorous as the juniper."

Don Pablo to Abel: "Abel, you don't have the sacrum of Osirus; life is a depraved burden of Tyre; if the will is feeble one is a noddle or a weather-headed, motherless changeling. I realize a woman can break a man into all the pieces of Charon's stygian boat, with one erotic grin. She has a weapon no wit can vanquish—her body. The boudoir must be a

bastion, and the husband, Cerberus, the
watchdog of the marriage bed. Suppose I'm a
cuckold; will the worms grieve more for me had
I a spouse, some soapy pots and pans, a
steadfast wife who genders indifferently?"

Dolly Patch: "Are you to be the cully of
Irish haunches?"

Don Pablo: "Is it better to be the sharper
than a dupe? Even a seer of a reverend book
was likely to sow horns when he was alive.

"Do I prefer a virgin or a whore? The
former is too inexperienced to cuckold you and
the latter too weary of the sport. Aristotle was
entombed with his harlot and his wife buried
with his possessions."

Dolly Patch: "Why aren't you catechizing
Lais? What is this locust doing at Palma every
weekend?"

Don Pablo: "A dispute with a woman is a
nervous disorder."

Dolly: "I suppose nothing will undo Brother
Pablo save a knot of pleasant news."

Doña Siegfrieda, beside herself, sank into a
dirge: "Where is the larva? Have they taken
him away knotted in his winding sheet?" She
screamed, brought out a bedpan with two

ounces of blood in it, and again ran into the house.

Don Pablo, not seeing his deranged wife, spoke to Abel: "What really troubles you? You're bookish, but several pieces of a simpleton. Had you my snowy, Alpine foibles I might advise you. However, I realize that one lesson sires countless lessons, and not is the parent of learning. People always commit the same drabbish errors, but conceit their latest nonsense is a brand new elephant blunder."

Abel: "I have sighed in vain to amount to something only to realize that something is nothing. More tranquil as a solitary, I am certain to embrace a person, for whom I do not care a whit; and after this dunghill chagrin I epitaph my heart."

Don Pablo gave Patch a sere eye. "Patch, you've misread the seers. But the real masterpiece of inanity is you. You're a pedantic doctor of booby knowledge."

Dolly: "Shrive my soul, if I'm not well-read, perhaps I'm a mere halfpenny of you."

Don Pablo: "Learning is the ornament of a man's nature and not his character."

Dolly: "Since we were boys you were a

whoremaster. At sleepy Torquay, a nursing
home for senile businessmen, you pillaged a
damaged uterus. You ever hankered for as
many bawds as there are mollusks in Tyre."

Don Pablo: "You do well, Dolly, to suck up
the humours of your smallness."

Dolly: "Your epicurism gives me nausea of
the heart. Always riggish, your sole motive was
to defile nipples, pink as the almond buds of a
Majorcan February."

Don Pablo: "The difference betwixt acute
pleasure and wild pain is no more than the
space of a groan. Grievous are all earthborn
men with puissant testicles."

Dolly: "A speculative sophism but what can
flesh that is ruined as a mastabah of Heliopolis
do with a salt harlot?"

Abel: "Lais is a riddle in Sumer. Whatever I
do for her seems to be the cause of her ill
nature. Lais is always packing her clothes and
going nowhere; then of a sudden she complains
of a megrim. She always wants to go away and
becomes ill thinking of it."

Don Pablo was rambling: " 'Tis best for a
woman to keep all the countries of the earth at
home. A damsel who travels is sure to forget

her suitcase in one room, her cosmetics and hairpins elsewhere, and her maidenhead in some town. It's futile making a journey because fleeing is the same as standing still."

Don Pablo: "Were man sane he would become no one. Patch, do you allege that such humdrum words as 'virtue,' 'honesty,' 'good deeds,' were invented by men who, you imply, don't have speaking genitals?"

Dolly grew fierce. "Your insight is smutted barley. No Hymen will carry torches for an antlered bridegroom. After your nuptials she'll lie as far from you as the Antipodes. At midday, following her marriage-night, she'll hang out the bridal sheets, stained with several drops of blood that issued from a pelting wound she made in her small finger with a penknife. Fossil brother, right now you're a memorial archive of a thousand cuckolds. So you're to have two wives? Are not a brace of women in a man's house an Amazonian legion? After she pillages you, she will disappear like a sirocco. It's cinnamon, asphaltus, myrrh, and the fume of myrrh of a chit with blossoming calves that blasts your intellect. Open your eyes; you think she's a mild trade wind that'll ease you. Take a

clear look at this Semiramis whose crib was peat
moss, and carrying cattle mash."

Pablo did not hear his apish mummer and
said to Abel: "Do you have thin nights? My
slumber is as deep as lost and sunk as Atlantis."

Abel: "I fear to sink into sleep, the mucoid
sister of death."

Dolly screamed, "By Bacchus, what a pair of
major gudgeons. I tell you, all men are insane
because they have privates. Lais the trull is
adroit as Poppaea Sabina."

Lais returns with the Tears of the Virgin to
garnish her hair.

Don Pablo engaged Lais. "Lais, you've had
humble experiences with slips in a frank,
plucking margaritas, and breaking Irish turf.
My myrtle, have you ever read a book?"

Lais's immaculate teeth were Don Pablo's
orison. "No, sir, I've been informed that a man
is far more useful than the most learned
volume."

Don Pablo, who laughed as seldom as Plato,
was mirthful. "What a wag you are. But one
receives rare pleasure from reading."

Lais frowned. "But isn't a book a rather
comfortless and dry bed?"

Don Pablo: "Lais, has no man ever broached your lilied vessel?"

Perplexed with Don Pablo's query, she answered, "Isn't that work for a publican?"

Don Pablo replied, "Doubtless he could also perform the labor, my seraph."

Abel had been preparing to leave above an hour, and he attempted a good-by. "Don Pablo, I must perforce go. Millennial apologies to you, noble sir. I'm restless as Lucifer, but would to God I could wake like the Morning Star."

Lais had gone into the house and returned with an alabaster box of the ointment of spikenard. She removed Don Pablo's shoes and socks, and anointed his feet.

Don Pablo: "Lais, I hear that Abel is his own prey, but is he yours, too? Poor Abel, he's a zany with any female; while a cormorant gamp was wantoning in his pockets he'd be terror-stricken at her lickerous motives."

Lais: "Isn't that a midwife? Are you jesting? Do you mean Abel's big with child? I'm always civil but Abel is so bookish and looks as though he were wearing grave clothes. Imagine a gawk like Abel with a light-heeled jill who's looking for easy gingerbread."

Don Pablo: "Does a good man bore you?"

Lais: "No, sir; unless he's too good to be a man. I guess a poulterer can pluck a chick far more easily than poor, kind Abel."

Then Lais kissed Don Pablo's turbulent veined hand and noiselessly departed.

Dolly watched this in a great amaze, his Adam's apple shaking as though it were about to drop from the branch of Sodom. "What of Doña Siegfrieda who pampers up your freakish fancies?"

"I buried Doña Siegfrieda last Friday. Abel, have you had sexual commerce with Lais?"

"She lies and lies, but not beneath me."

Dolly was overjoyed. "She would comfort those in the graveyard were they not content to lie where they are. A murrain on your Aphrodite! Lais is an anemone who's already at the fag end of her jaded April."

Don Pablo turned again to Abel. "My own hopes are bedrid mummies. I'm implacably senseless, but still assume the bed is cates, ale, and wastel bread. Sin-eater, antique of Egypt, how many obelisks and pylons have perished within me? I tasted the grave as a boy. After the primy age of seven all flesh is depraved. But sin

is older than the world; I suppose that I could
be cured by a babe's urine, nature's balsam.
True, I cannot remember a Lenten week, yet
had I not been a fool with women, I would have
been a fool without them. We die with all our
sins entire; we are water, air, fire, and earth,
riveted together by Eros and Doom. The world
is dead. I speak since I am able to talk about
nothing better than anybody else."

Abel modestly declined his lissom neck.
"Occasionally when I consider the lilies of the
matrix, I diet on dry water, cracknels, and a
musked eventide. Could I gloze, my suns would
not be jet black nor the hours my scaffold."

Dolly Patch's Adam's apple appeared to be
on the leeward side of his neck. "Brother, take
her to the gardens at Cheapside to physic her
with herbs. I have a suspicion that's gall in my
angelic heart she's worse than the plague of
1603 in the suburbs of London, notorious for
piacular whores. What would you have with
her, a hedge-marriage?"

Don Pablo, weary, gave his whole attention
to Abel. "My hours are the manna that grow by
night and stink by noon. My passions have aged
among the palms in the wilderness of Engedi. Is

and was are the same, and ultimately nothing.
What else can I do except itch for venery or the
grave? Abel, why are you such a gull?"

Abel: "Don Pablo, my heart is a common
street through which Mr. and Mrs. Villain
Little may pass and drop their petit bourgeois
offals."

Dolly had not exhausted his fribble-frabble.
"Have you not heard that Lais goes every
Friday to Palma and sits at the outdoor Bar
Formentor? Though she is solitary, her womb
is not. Afar, I thought she was a gammer with
her legs agape, wearing whorish eye shadow
beneath her eyelids."

Don Pablo continued to bridle his mouth,
but he answered: "She does not use the cheap
powder and wormwood rouge of a drab of Ur.
Abel, what do *you* really know of Lais O'Shea?"

"Actually nothing except that she troubles
my aspen pulse."

Dolly interrupted. "Lais's patron saint is
Julia, who will permit every man a snug night's
lodging."

Dolly, observing a botch of ire on Don
Pablo's neck, began to dance and chant:
"You've bestowed upon Lais twelve coal mines,

a vasty emporium in Chelsea, and 70,000
shares in Yorkshire cotton mills, whilst the
ninny, Abel, buys her stockings and
amber-colored petticoats and skirts that shine
like the gold of Ophir. Poor, fond Brother who
dotes on the peakish vixen, hear the psalmodic
warning of the Hebrew prophet to vainglorious
ancient Israel:
    'Tell it not in Gaza,
    Say it not in Gath,
    Lest the daughters of the Philistines
rejoice.' "

    "May I sleep while you dip your spleen in
hyssop? Dolly, you're a sea-hare, a bane to
others and to itself. I've been sore wasted by
gamps, bawds, jades, and slatterns. But as I
breathe beneath the Majorcan sky, she will not
receive a pence from me except posthumously.
Ah, Abel, you're too mild to decoy me."

    "No, sir, not while I have a better cony,
myself. It is a parable, and a sore perplexing
one, that though I am mild, and mildly
inoffensive, that the juice of mulberries was
used to incite the elephants at Antioch to
battle."

    Don Pablo: "May the music of the estuaries

and the feathery heavens ease my spirit.
Besides, I deny my own existence, the globe is
dispeopled, and as apocryphal as time and space.
It is not sagacity, but the want of it, that allows
us our vagaries. Nobody can know his own
nature and live."

Don Pablo added: "Perhaps no woman can
purge my humours. Don't carp upon Lais
O'Shea; one may expect a crop of calumny
during the fall and the summer solstice. Slander
appears, of a sudden, like the early morning
mushroom."

Dolly: "Women commonly forget
everything except calumny which she deposits
in her vulva until it rots. Have you noticed a
vine turning away to avoid the offensive
cabbage? O grandiose fool, I'll wager she's
barren too."

Don Pablo: "Thyme blows on the sterile
hillocks. Though the branches of my arms and
trunk are decayed, the root of me still
simmers."

Dolly howled, "So you still imagine you'll be
groaning like the mandrake!"

Pablo's hymn was simple: "I shall bruise her
nipples until they are odoriferous as calamus. I

will sacrifice two tawny orange heifers at the
phallic altar of Baalpeor to restore my
generative force."

Pablo closed his rugose eyelids and fell into a
billowy slumber. Dolly and Abel, accustomed to
vapor a great deal, left, the former going to an
outdoor café for cognac and the latter entering
No Hay Nada. Abel purged his nostrils with
rue. The stench issued from the *torrente* into
which Don Bartolomé's workmen cast the
rabbits after skinning them; that granite
channel built by the Moor before the Rood had
been planted in Majorca was the houndes' ditch
of the pueblo.

Don Bartolomé walked softly beneath the
arbor at the Villa D'Or. Then, on tiptoe past
the well, he espied the pair of carpenters who
were carrying a coffin wrought of the trunk of
an olive tree. He queried the two *obreros*, "Don
Pablo is dos metros, talvez poco mas?"

"Si, si, Don Bartolomé!"

They laid the wooden room for the corpse *on
the granite floor*. Don Pablo sat at the edge of
the patio in his Roman curule chair.

Don Bartolomé was wearing summer shorts,
although the branches were scarce leafing.

Don Pablo awoke. "Don Bartolomé, have
you no shame? The dignity of an aged man lies
not in his naked, burly legs, but in his brows.
What, pray, is this timber? Are you hiring these
obreros to build a scaffold for you?
Woolly-headed gawk of cupidity, why cumber
your benefactor already nigh unto the grave?"

"O Don Pablo, it was my devout, Catholic
resolve to furnish you a chamber gorged with
Arabian gums that expel the worm that tickles a
corse more adroitly than a prostitute."

Don Pablo viewed the coffin and, resting his
herculean chin upon his shaggy, animal hands,
said, "How couth you are, Bartolomé. Begone,
saprogenic pate!"

Bartolomé, displaying the daubery of
meekness, knelt down, asked Don Pablo to
pardon him, and then left.

The *obreros* were already running away,
shouting, "A spectre! The skull of Golgotha!
Shall we sit and sup with a dead man, though
Christ, Mary, and Hanna know that we're
hungry?"

Don Antonio Mentira shortly thereafter was
present. Don Pablo was still spewing forth his

rancor: "Go now, Antonio, have you been in the public stews with Lais O'Shea?"

"I'm wived, with four children. The bawdy houses are in the alleys of Palma which are strange and alien to my honor." He placed his hand over his pettifogging heart, and leaving, said, "Mon honneur! Mon honneur!"

Dolly Patch came asking almost plaintively, "Brother, are you stepping into this siren's lair with your eyes open?"

"Dolly, could a man open his eyes before he was overwhelmed by a female, he'd never be passionate. Lubricious Nature has taught the female to change her face often as the skies are colored with antimony or daubed with mire on the marge of the Tigris. One seldom knows what is occurring until later. Maybe I can only be the Magellan of her mouth, circumnavigating it. Or engage in waggish pleasantries. Is not refined conversation with a young woman a form of coition?"

Dolly: "Excuse me, sir, your breath is piebald with hair tonic, face powder, and a man's barber's breath."

There is a bruit of Lais said to be gravid as

the mullet. At once Don Bartolomé sent Don
Pablo a basket of apricots; the proprietor of El
Colmado arrived to fame Don Pablo as a
machiavel with women and left him a supper of
toasted sea urchins mixed with oak galls and
spiced with leaves of the yew. Don Antonio
gave him a piscatorial handshake. And Teasing
Urlington, age eighty-three, whose nose was
long as a pike fish and who had purchased
batteries connected with a modesty-vest to
rejuvenate her womb, gave Don Pablo an
unexpected electric shock.

Doña Siegfrieda issued from the darksome
bowels of the house, and beckoned with her
hand to Mercedes to take hold of Don Pablo's
arm on one side while she held the other. It was
time to change his swaddling clouts.

 PART III

Doña Siegfrieda was in her privy chapel; in the middle was a table with two lighted candles between which was a porcelain cockerel, painted red, the feet resting on a golden ball. Posted against the wall was a drawing of a solar Osiris; next it was the bull, Scrapis.

There was a lithograph of Christ with a vermillion logoscomb of a cockerel, another of Jesus with an Ass's head. Also a design of Hermes-Logos in the shape of a rooster with an upright, feathered tail. Hard by it was the Cock in the Garden of Eden beneath which was inscribed: "In the beginning was Logos, the Word, and the Word was made phallus, the second person of the Holy Trinity."

On a poster was a white, leg-horned
Christ-Rooster, and alongside it a
Logos-Priapus crucified.

Doña Siegfrieda held the New Testament in
her hand while gaping at a poster of a cock. She
vaguely recollected that quack diviner Abel, a
mish-mash of understanding, hare-brained
crotchets, who, like a hawker, carried about his
neck on a string a crucible and a chapbook of
Paracelsian remedies and was always ailing; his
most recent malaise was the Jew-baiting Gospel
according to John and the crazy scribblings of
Paul, a perverted profligate and Israelite, as he
alleges.

The bumpkin, Abel, asserted that The
Word, spite of John's Gnostic sensibilities,
never became flesh. Doña Siegfrieda, who
abhorred Hitler, could never swallow the feral
accusations that Jews who stoned a malefactor,
one who ravished a virgin or housewife, a
murderer, ever crucified a sinner.

Nor does Josephus, a turncoat Jew, who
prized the friendship of Titus, and who detailed
sundry false Messiahs, have any cause to omit
Christ. The Gnostic argument was that it was

The Word, thirsting for its own glory, that
asked for water and was offered vinegar and
hyssop by a Roman.

Her muddled head was a grief; why was she
concerned with Jew-baiting John? Doña
Siegfrieda read at random Paul's crazy Epistle
to the Romans: "For that which I do I allow
not: for what I would, that do I not; but what I
hate, that do I." Is this a precept of a devout
religious? Then what evidence is there in the
Old Testament that Abraham, who slept
beneath the oak of Mamre and had a seraphic
vision, was a fornicator, and that Isaac, who had
a vacant cranium, was pensive?

Did not Jesus, or The Word, inform Peter,
who handled the weir, and was born under the
constellation of Pisces, the Fishes, that he
would disown The Word thrice before the
Logos-cock crowed. At ninety-two Don Pablo
was still an old rounder who had several vials of
Jewish blood in his veins, and was not this the
cause of her obsession. The Gospels are
pseudography: There are twelve signs of the
Zodiac; twelve tribes of Israel; twelve sons of
Jacob; and twelve imaginary disciples unknown

to the four anti-Semetic scribes, and whose
scrowe is unbelievable. Are Jews always to be
annihilated for a man who never existed?

Doña Siegfrieda tore off all her garments,
hurled her marcasite rings that
penny-pack-father, husband Don Pablo, had
given her with such an air of grace, and stood
naked in her private oratory. She wailed aloud,
and viewing a chanticleer with reverence,
genuflected and sang an orison: "It is the Last
Supper of the Logos."

The door was slightly ajar and Mercedes,
observing this pagan, Gnostic ritual, crossed
herself and fled.

On the patio El Medico observed Doña
Siegfrieda's tallowish jowl. In her two hands
was a chalice smeared with gore which she
alleged she found every day beside Don Pablo's
bed. Her moans were as hoarse as a roaring sea
against a shingle. El Medico fingered her jaw
that dwarfed her dry ovaries, suggesting also a
touch of lycanthropy, for which he prescribed
two tenth deals of an umbellifer boiled with
pulse and flour. As a result of widow madness
he said she might take at dawn St. James his
Wort, a physic for green wounds.

Don Pablo, who had fallen from his chair and suffered a luxation, told Señor Patch to go to the apothecary for the crushed roots of a reed swimming in vinegar and to apply it as a plaister to Don Pablo's hip.

Lais beheld Don Pablo who roared: "Have you been running about with that brothel, Felix Mandeza or drinking San Miguel beer with the wheezy gammer Teaser Urlington? Adultery is a canker that eats the jealous heart until it's too raw to bud another spring. Go and drop a tear over Doña Siegfrieda's grave."

Lais brought him a cup of tea, and said: "Thank you, sir."

Don Antonio came and when he saw Doña Siegfrieda and Don Pablo he tried to disappear; but Doña's shirtwaist was open, and he stood there consuming her skin. Doña Siegfrieda pulled him up short: "What's he left me, a widowhood?"

"Don Juan Ladrone is studying it in Palma; I disremember Don Pablo's latest codicil. 'Mon honneur, I swear, and if I lie, may I never sleep with my wife again.'"

He broke out into a decayed smile that came from his levantine teeth.

"Antonio, I know your false peseta smile,
and don't mention to me your nasty bedroom
life."

Don Antonio took another oath. "Mon
honneur, I agree, a man's a worm in bed," and
he vanished.

Near his winding sheet, Pablo's spectral past
was burning snow covering the crumbly veins
and the fevered blains of his tottering mind.
Suddenly, he noticed Lais had disappeared. He
heard the sound of the Paracelsian electrum of
the adulterer. The crookback *Abogado* Antonio
Mentira who was rushing headlong from Lais's
bed in the servants' quarters of Villa Alegra?

Though Dolly was seated in the granitic
patio, Pablo supposed he was in town guzzling
vino corriente. His cold mind wandered,
piecemeal, through Orcus; then suddenly called
aloud to his bondservant, Dolly: "Bury me on
the old stony slopes of Israel. Inject my
fundament with the balsam of a tree of Jericho
to preserve it from spoil, and clothe my
exsiccative mummy with the lawn of a bishop's
sleeve piebald with Egyptian flax, or bury me
close to the cataracts of Karnak with a stele

bearing a pittance of my shrunken name I had
mistaken for fame. Pour oil upon a cairn of
stones and hide me with the fat soil of On. Set
my ashes in an urn fragrant with the oil of iris.
Raise a funeral pile of olive wood with the
moiety of a small basaltic hill. Let me not waste
away beneath a stupid rood muttering in the
maggot-eaten rain, or fouled by a tomb made
for a hewer of water.

"I have drunk up myriads of shrunken nights
and lay in a stupor until bastard saffron
daybreak shone on my face. Think of all the
English towns—Kent, Plymouth, Dover,
Devon, York—meadows honeycombed with
grain fields and splashed with a viscid mere
fringed with highway purslane. How cloying
were my days when there was no siren in a
kersey with toadstool nipples to assuage my rue.

"Inhume my bones nearby Sidon, for old
graves fame our lives. Know I will not be
slimed in limbo or under a commoner's crucifix
who killed up his meager dim-lit soul washing
out spittoons. And feed the gorbelly explosion
with olive, pine, and silver fir of oleaceous
Lebanon, and throw into the blaze, Bartolomé.

Lard the animal combustion with my cuckold,
Antonio Mentira, and nourish it with his
putrescent nose.

"May the animal hunger of my flames
shaped like the boat of Isis not be pestered with
too many corpses. I pray my thirsted flame be
not kinless, but be fed with the bowels, liver,
bladder, and kidneys of Dolly. Find seven dogs,
all bitches, to eat him in a combustible pyramid.
Hurl the Proprietor of El Colmado into the
greedy fire that I may amerce him for his
arcane of comestibles and the obese debts I owe
him. Reduce him to memorial clinkers and the
crocus of Mars. May the Lord God spare my
incontinent remains, and keep them entire that
they be not the cause of a lewd guffaw.

"Where is my cockbrained memory? Can not
the learned doctor of physic increase my
furious, avenging blaze?

"Should the detritus of my decease be
consumed in an orphaned obituary? I forbid the
moor, diarrhoeal Leandro, and *criada* Mercedes
with the sardine mouth to attend my corse.
Stuff the funeral pile with five mucous nuns
that it may smack of Majorca. Should Dolly fail
to be consumed, kick him along with a burro

and a wily mongrel into the furnace of my
ghost.

"This is my brimstony testament and entire
bequest to all No Hay Nadans. Were I to leave
my fortune to be massacred, Ingratitude would
continue, since thanks is an archangel but not
of this world. I know the sweet, vasty throne
upon which is seated Gramercy. Who will pay
heed to the kind, pitying grass that clothes the
naked mendicant bones in the earth?"

After hearing this, Dolly spoke to El Medico
Muchas Pesetas, *Abogado* Antonio Mentira and
the Proprietor of El Colmado that his brain-sick
brother was determined that they join him in
his ultimate fiery sepulcher.

El Medico left his alchemy genius to muse
upon the entangled mischief of Don Pablo.
Awakening, he announced he would cook a
noxious broth in his laboratory that would
despatch their false, slipper patron, Don Pablo.
Adoring his skill as an awesome apothecary
chef, El Medico delivered this declamation to
the three kindly laymen who expressed much
astonishment: "Don Pablo, a military tactician
who has ambushed Death will now be taught
not to snare us. Heed me, this is the decoction I

have in mind: hog gum from the West Indies, pieces of a hippopotamus of Barbary, the lepry juice of eight dragons taken with the sop Christ gave Judas."

Don Bartolomé, no less impressed than the others, but still unsettled, was ready to assault his own human goodness ill-used by Pablo. Were not thousands of decades of honest ordure, conveyed in carts each year to Pablo's groves, at least worth a Pyrenean tin-mine?

Abogado Antonio Mentira could not recollect Don Pablo's variegated supplements to his benefactions; could an upstart *abogado* at Puerto de Pollenso have added one more pedantical footnote to the becrazed man's will? Maybe the testament had been so amended as to reward that stormy, weather-bitten vagina, Lais. The four stood on the Plaza, each more senseless than the other.

Reaching no conclusion, Dolly returned to Villa D'Or and pleaded with his brother Pablo, saying everyone was a mawworm; he admitted he had been a foolhardy unthrift. And that his fragile inly nature was torn asunder by a brother closer to the kinless winds than to him. Dolly stated he could no longer bear such

high-stomached indigence. And that he, no less
than the daughters of Babylon, had sat in the
dust whilst this crocus bearing the toy title of
Don Pablo burned for moldering stockings and
sandals or any tarnished dove.

And Dolly bellowed: "When did I starve
your largesse to salve my penury? You deemed
yourself the pippin-mime of the *Iliad*s by
reciting the deeds of Achilles before you
scambled up enough valor to nibble the chemise
of a jillet attired by a slop clothier. Can you feel
how it is to be a chaste virgin? You ate my
honor raw for any pastime with a bawd or a
shuffling houri clad in a dress trimmed with
miniver. You humbled my tongue and gave me
dreggy oil and Majorcan bread for my meals. In
this unhoused world, I am more in the other.

"I've been the sumpter-ass bearing the load
of your subtlety. O my Pride is dear to my
bones and no she-scavenger has ever chewed
them, for I have walked barefoot in my own
uncuckolded Dignity. Do you know shame,
Pablo, how it is to own nothing except a frigid
mendicancy of four lustra? Do you know how
icy and hungry is poverty? Have you ever
waited for a supper of breadless penury?"

Dolly continued: "Presently I shall disclose to you an enchiridion containing a medley of mildewed wives, sundry brachs garbed in marry-muff; and a guinea-hen whose abode was a back-house. There was a gamp who, whenever she stirred, stabbed her dress with her own bones. Then what lubricious delight you took inhaling her sour kelpy breath. You've langourously chewed your ninety-two years of dowds, stale forced, meats, as a scholiast goes from one leaf to another of Langland or Pausanias. You itched for a scrawny pullet, or trimmed a refined moneylender of 100-pound sterling so that you could nibble the poached teats of a bawd's daughter. Later you were overcome by a foetid spinster with the hoot of an owl. Any female gutterblood inflated your covetous animal arms."

Don Pablo attempted to constrain Dolly's invective that was like insects fretting the integument of his craw: "What are all of us but a choir of worms?"

Dolly: "Only Doña Siegfrieda has been your virgin spouse."

Don Pablo: "Buffoon of my ruins, miscalled

knowledge, do not allude to my pious Siegfrieda
lest she howl in her tomb."

Dolly: "Nobody venerates a beggar with a
torn pair of breeches and chinks in his shoes."

Dolly: "Who troubles naked Poverty save a
knot of ravaging crows? I've been homeless
everywhere, an exile in your pack-penny
pockets, a vault for smoked whores,
chip-and-fish shopgirls.

"You slyly sacked a maidenhead in the foul
industrial gut of Bristol. You regarded yourself
a volcanic rhetor of the uterus. How is it
possible for a dowd to conycatch a seer simply
because she has a cranny between her legs? And
I thought true learning was not between or
betwixt, but was of the highest altitude."

Don Pablo: "Patch, you suppose a man of
any age knows what he's doing? He's no less a
gullish infant at three or at ninety-two. Were it
in the power of a human being to consent to
enter the world, he wouldn't do it. Were I kind
to you, you would claim I'd flea'd you until you
were dead."

Dolly: "Brother Pablo, what canting,
bootless nonsense. Do you allege you're kind or

that your heart was ever stung with agenbite?
You're amiable, but that's just a sociable
pigment on your cheeks. I detest a man with a
pleasing disposition who's only pleasing himself.
But I agree, all I've learned that is bad comes
from you; it's wry that virtue is never one's
mistress. I may be a small-sized droll, but no
butcher of your secondhand lusts. God, how
nature spoils our dwarfy loins, and worse, our
dwindled intellect."

Don Pablo: "Patch, each even-tide I wear a
shroud called Night and that's the closest to
Truth I'll ever be."

Dolly: "On All Saints' Day we went together
to the charnel. Your eyes were a tear-bottle.
The sole female you ever declined was the town
pawnbroker, Margarita Concepción, who sells
dolls of Mary, Martha, Ignatius Loyola, and
that little woeful cuckold, Joseph. What you
abhorred was not her shallow neck or spavined
shanks, but her starched shift, her newly
laundered corset, and her soapy chemise,
symptoms of her stiff Catholic morals."

Don Pablo: "I'd even glut your dog-faced
truisms. Homunculus, you don't gender

because you have a sham nose that can neither smell what's good or bad."

Dolly: "Think on the time we went together to the town charnel-house filled with rows of roods that resembled gallows, that covered all the thick-skulled martyrs duped by the hollow-hearted passions of a popinjay. Protestant, I can't stomach the heathen relics, the body of Prima, the remains of St. Monica, the chambermaid or whore Magdalen who doubtless poxed the Galilean fishers. I don't care a pin for hagiolatry."

Dolly: "There is no sporting-house vast enough to contain your Academe of harlots. He who confessed you is himself a wencher of No Hay Nada. How could you bring down your sole kindred bones for a rapacious chit whose nipples had been toasted by the putrid breaths of riff-raff rogues. What's the glory, really, in shameless dirt? Do you sanctify an imposthume or a pimple vermillion as a ruby?"

Don Pablo: "A novice Catholic, I can't understand the Gentile Pharisee preaching on the sacred writings of the Old Testament and determined to depart the cote of ancient Israel.

I would cry out: 'Raze the Vatican to the
ground!' were it not I knew that were that
unborn edifice demolished the state would
become the church.

"See whether I err: The Spanish idolaters,
who are mad for corpses, built a pile of Gothic
stones, a marvel to behold, but should all who
are not Christians be immolated for heaps of
hard-wrought rocks?"

Don Pablo continued: "I know you're a
fourth-blooded kin without a spermal nose.
What need of toy saints has the voracious race
of men? Of St. George who sold porkers? Zeno
castrated himself, but did he burn the less for a
prostitute? Hippolytus was torn asunder by
horses which is a pagan legend. I'm not pining
away for the dust of a pinchbeck canonized
puppet in a crypt at Poitier, or St. Agnes and
the stupid lamb at her feet, or Barbara who
protects religious dunderheads against
lightning. What of that lunatic Benedict who
repels devils that are the genitals of satyrs.
Long ago it was Paul, Hebrew of the Hebrews,
and a turncoat Pharisee, who had the falling
sickness; on the road to Damascus he feigned
he had seen Christ, a Word, who has spilled two

thousand centuries of blood of the exilic Jew.

"Did St. Hiliary, patron of snakes, free the English of the plague in 1515? What do we do with St. Gertrude? We hold a festival in her honor March 17 because at that season she drove field mice from their hibernaculum and destroyed them. Can we be saved from our frail grass and sepulchers by Cyriac who announced he was a Christian at the age of three and who was hurled down the steps and died? Am I to batten on such foolery? Is this not new-fangled insanity? Then there's St. Eugenia. Her relics were celebrated until Emperor Constantine threw them into the sea. Or Catherine of Siena who wears a nimbus of thorns.

"My mind is stored with a jumble of conceits lately come by in my green meadows of dotage. And who is Ethelburga, foundress of an abbey; maybe her rib is in a sarcophagus at Kent. You'll blame me for my exhausted infidel faith for not wailing at the graves of inhumed spouses, paramours, or a flock of drossy teated girls. Their burial sites were a gynaecaum for grubs and the sod. I cannot be a motley by shedding tears for extinct cadavers.

"A No Hay Nadan at the charnel on All

Saints' Day is a Spanish heathen madman.
What have I to do with the Furies who run
about from one slab to another? On All Saints'
Day the motive of the parents was to shake up a
coil and to muzzle their children, ruffian
hagseeds, who wore necklaces of biscuits and
comfits with which they stuffed themselves
while a grandsire or wife long past her seed
time bawled and wept. Would not such a
tawdry show of feeling cloy the bowels?"

Dolly: "A moribund colossus, you pointed
out the tombstones that concealed a fay or a
guileless dame you once ransacked.

"How many vials of virgin milk were soured
by your thunder? A braggart actor, you showed
me the graves of unwed parlor maids you had
sacked as if you were a pursy coltish Antony.
Where are the plump festival knees now under
the idolatrous marl of No Hay Nada, the
ground of Kent, the Isle of Wight, Hong Kong,
Bangkok, Ceylon, the Hebrides, Jamaica,
Samoa?

"Did you ever grieve for a leman now a skull
for snakes and lizards? O, the hapless
adulteresses and the jilted oven wives of grum
grocers, tinkers and pewterers, fullers, mercers,

chandlers from East Cheape or Grass Street or the soke of Liverpool."

Don Pablo: "Had I one jot of heaven's gift, I would have been a marriage broker of the Muse or a Calybite lodged in a hut. I understand that the sensation of venery is not much different from peeling a scab or a ringworm."

Dolly: "Judas betrayed Christ for a kiss and you for the loins of toothy sluts and the uliginous dugs. You composed a palinode versifying your specious regrets for pillaging sundry marriage-beds of a continent tinker, an ascetic baker, a steadfast machinist. You were an adroit Hannibal of Carthage who sacked honeycombed Italy of its lilied damsels, virgin nieces of Roman senators, and stable wives of pelf. Never satiated, you posed as a Machiaval offering wedlock to a wealthy dissolute grass-widow, a proprietor of a large dry goods store, a humid spinster who owned four bawdy-houses, a wild pigeon who had prostituted her fleshy frame for a wheat and barley farm outside the Midlands, and a voracious madam who had inherited nine fruit orchards in Warwickshire. Thus, you garnered up an immense fortune and anointed your name

by erecting a home for orphan girls brought to
bed with child whose fathers had vanished in
New Zealand, the Isle of Wight, and the
British Bahamas. You even donated a ward to a
Catholic nursing home for bachelors
recuperating from prostate surgery and
venereal diseases and paid for the plaque on
which is inscribed: 'In honor of Gentleman
Percival Williams, a devout adorer of Our
Saviour.'

"Hear, foul whoremaster, the dirge of Edith
Sweethams, Myrtle Achingfoot, Agnes So
Easy, Maureen Too Kind, Virgin Bertha
Livesoft buried in poor kendal with an honest
besom at her side, Anne Sincere Loose,
Catherine Ne Touchez Pas, Joan Very Polite,
Beryl Godsend, Evelyn Bedstead, Roberta
Windfall, Helen Meager Head, Laura Longing,
Sibyl Maidenhead, died in childbed, Margaret
Jovial Navel, immaculate daughter of Henry
Jovial Navel, alderman of Manchester, 1902."

Dolly Patch continued his humbug encomia
of the dead: "Irma Soothing, virgin daughter of
Albert Soothing, baker and Mayor of Kent,
1900; Rachel Blessing T'All, 1903, void of any
kin or husband; Nancy Goodbottom, deceased

1907, honest spinster; Maid Ethel
Hedge-Tavern, expired of extreme celibacy,
1906."

Momentarily, Dolly paused to stay his
scoffing memorial: "Mary Hospitable Cranny,
daughter of Scrupulous Miller Cranny, Kent,
1910; *Señora* Muchos Hombres, barren as
Rachel but with a supple figure, 1914; *Señorita*
Carolina Toledo y Mala; Consuela Sevilla
Malsonante; Helen Bedlove; Angela Dearfoot;
Asposia Poltfoot; Maria Robión Roca y
Sencillo; Jerónima Galleta Chulo; Señorita
Virgen Carmelita y Constancia, expired
delivering a buxom infant; Felicia Ulmo y
Tucca, *hija* of *Padre* Henrado Benedict Ulmo y
Tucca; Saracen Mescla Castidád Malagro,
muerto 1913, No Hay Nada."

Don Pablo: "Mite of forceless evil, habits
good or ill, loosely bind people together. A
skeleton of my quondam phallic strength, I
grow old and puke in my dish of gruel and
seventh nonage.

"You're covetous, a virgin liar, false as
marcasites; you furtively steal my pesetas for
cognac, bite my back, neck, arms, and offer me
daily chop-logic, and I despise all of your

defects. One could be fond of a man with the same pitchy faults provided he was not Patch."

Dolly: "Before you were Don Pablo you were Percival Williams of Kent. I cringe when I observe your prim household mincing. You'd be a mealy babe were you not an apple-sodom. I'm downright splenetic. I show my worms in the sun, and my artless rot in the rain."

Don Pablo: "No one can minish a mooncalf."

Dolly: "My beginnings were more plain than yours; bankrupt, a constant but honest unthrift I was not accustomed to your knacks of avoiding the catchpole. Released from debtors' prison, I walked from Manchester to Liverpool with only a suit of threadbare flax to hide my shameless indigence. I've no gullet for your gawds nor any talent in gnawing creditors piecemeal. I'm naive, and the Levantine is a rabble hypocrite in every latitude. His diet on sparrows brought in from littoral Vigo and that hang by strings in the *carnicería* make my gorge rise. After you've licked the pork chops clean, Leandro takes them to his dampish wife who uses them for *sopa Mallorquina*."

Don Pablo: "The padre and the rich see to it

that the *obrero* takes the vow of poverty. The
workmen are martyrs whose skin is flayed no
less than St. Lewis. A Majorcan *obrero* is born
to be a moldy Lazarus and he'll die one.
There's nothing to feed a fowl; no gull flies
over this isle of hunger. A Majorcan is a liar
and thief at birth and a more seasoned one in
his bier."

Dolly Patch continued: "Brother, let's die in
English Kent, on the rough, gnarled shore by
the woody sea."

Don Pablo: "I used to give the Moor
Leandro a *propina* of five centimes, but how do
you know you're not hindering a man by aiding
him? All kindness is a buffoon's act; Leandro
looks at night for snails, sorrel, celery, and
parsley. Whenever I've given him a glass of
cognac he assumes I'm just another peregrine
dupe. One can't do anything for anybody
without spoiling his character.

"I don't deny my drabbing. All our sins are
entire in the womb; the rest of us lies in alien
countries. A man's vows, though straight and
without any clandestine purpose, are too sly for
flesh. Dolly, you were a dingthrift in grubby
Manchester when you were fobbing your

creditors. In Devon, a nursing home for retired
usurers, gunsmiths, and spindled spinsters, I
rescued you from the bumbailiff. You think I
was such an abstruse doctor of lechery. It's the
manly experience. No matter, am I to
excogitate my winding sheet while everyone
befools me? Suppose I mistook Madam
Pantry-Respect of Bath for an unspotted matrix
from Homer's fair-haired town of Achaia. Do
you believe women ransack your pockets for
spiders and moths. How barren one feels when
nobody thinks you're not even worth duping. I,
too, have suffered alone beneath the moist
constellation of the Fishes, Pisces, without a
woman's consoling arms or couth mouth to
make my blood sing.

"A man who's never been in woman trouble
has a meacock prepuce. Long ago my keel was
champed by seaworms. When you sojourned at
Sheffield, town of nuts and bolts and steel, you
were the ostrich who ate up metals—zinc,
platinum and stones—you were your own
tornado of penury."

Dolly: "Now that you're at your end, you
garnish your evil adventures with agate and
jacinth as if you were ornamenting your grave."

Don Pablo: "At Little East Cheape you were an apprentice butcher, and you never comprehended the difference between sweetbread or the decayed pudding a muleteer takes in his wagon down to the dung boat on the Thames. Should I be mummified, and you had not a pence for coal, you'd break up my mummy for fuel. I lie awake all night and for a tumor of nothing. Bay the moon, but rever my stêle."

Don Pablo's rambling elocution could not be tethered: "My learning is a fribble, the veneration of words. It excites my pulse to know that alfalfa is of Arabic origin. When I hear that parsley was cultivated by Charlemagne, that plant becomes Holy Writ in my soul. But you, Patch, are a bastard mime of my trivial lore. Speak, and you vex my veins tender as the anemone quaking in the wind. An herbalist who reveals that colewort drunk with wine drives away serpents teaches me what to do with my own demons. Would that Abel, who peddles any nostrum better than El Medico's Gorgon pills, were here to mollify my underfoot spirit.

"Unable to discover an occupation for a

wastrel and a manling, I gave you leave to
return to East Cheape, garbed as an
herbwoman selling hedge hissop. Of a sudden
you believed you had swallowed a pint of sea
marsh; and I had you confined to a spittle.
Seaweeds anchor themselves to stones until
they can stand alone, but not Patch. For
afterwards, I must perforce set you up as an
apothecary in Kent; then your wife was
spermed by the ice man and the brat looked like
a dachshund. The Last Supper is ourselves. We
are furnished with peevish, stubble brains, and
all we can reap are a few grains of stunted
conjectures."

El Medico interrupted the colloquy,
considering how he could dissolve Doña
Siegfrieda's megrim. At Fornaluxt, her bulky
loins quailed, and in town she could not hide
Don Pablo's marital dishonor. The marl
between the granite of Villa D'Or was
crumbling. El Medico recommended that she
genuflect twelve times before Saint Genevieve
who would furnish her with mortar for the
house and meat and bread of her hungry
wedlock. Otherwise he prescribed six prayers a
day to Our Lady of Perpetua, three to St.

James of Compostello, and twenty-four aspirin smeared with the lard of a gelded pig drowned in muscadel.

Then Abel appeared, and El Medico beseeched the archangel Michael to slay this aspen lazar. As petitions to heaven are never heard, he mumbled: "He pines for a vixen, but flees her. He walks in fabric that chafes his senses. Perhaps his garments give him twinges that unsettle him. Jesus, Joseph, and Mary, everybody is dying and no one is dead."

El Medico: "A padre can bless a burro, but what can I, disciple of Holy Galen, do for you, Señor Abel?"

Abel: "Forgive me, El Medico, yesterday I discovered that if I had no anatomy it would never have troubled me."

El Medico: "I'm qualmish. I smell an ossuary."

Abel was no Titus to take the walls of Jerusalem, but he decided he might ambush this medical Gargantua of peregrine sputum with a touch of candor: "Sir, I belong to an earlier age that had a garnish of pomp and cypress, and am coffined in a kinless mob world."

Abel: "I realize I'm sunk outside the rabble cote."

El Medico: "Señor Abel, what am I able to do with a man whose cracked senses are the tinklings of a sheep; what can I do with a pile of ruined nerves?

I can't kiln you because you've fallen into a dotage or an archaic vocabulary."

Abel: "Like Gautier I love dictionaries, especially old ones. Why should I relinquish, though solely a reader, glorious four-letter words such as WORD, Zeus, JHVH, Isis, Adam, Seth, Shem, for Billingsgate? Shakespeare and Ben Jonson and Pope may be obsolete, but I prefer them to hideous neologisms that offend my ear. A seer may fail, and is still a wonder to our senses. Failure solely belongs to the seer, and the mediocrity cannot ever flesh his dullness."

Abel gasped, falling into an unheard declamation: "Can a quack speak as a seer? Ah, well, I'll never understand anybody.

"Would a caudle of cloves of the Moluccas be a nostrum for the lees of my sick October life? When I'm queasy, choleric, or in the dumps, I pound the flower of Brass adding to it a drachma of Saturn's lead and a scruple of an archaic lament, and I heat them in a limbeck, after which I have the most puzzling feelings. No doubt, all this is as worthless as dragon's blood."

When El Medico asked Don Pablo to quiet his wife's hagged nights, the valetudinary was bathing his stout, songless mouth in the four o'clock Majorcan skies. The physicmonger stood there lost in hilly-headed clouds. What ailed this Hagar, Doña Siegfrieda? Was her womb graved? Once more he looked at the penniless imp, Dolly Patch, and again glanced at that cock-brained Abel.

Abel: "I fear lakes, a toothless, crank stream, a gasping sheet of fretful water."

Don Pablo: "Maybe the bracing air of Nova Scotia might bind up my chanting arteries. But there are no heaths or moors in the New World, and I've heard that instead of thinkers, such aboriginal ground can only produce a parcel-poet."

El Medico said his rosary and departed.

At moon-tide, Don Pablo heard the tocsin of the Paracelsian electrum, and shouted he'd disinherit Antonio Mentira who was hurrying

away from Lais's bedstead in the *criada*'s
basement of Villa Alegra. At that instant Doña
Siegfrieda died.

Late morning Don Pablo was informed he
was a widower. He rubbed his columnar neck
until the igneous itch dimly recalled his spectral
conjugal frolics with Doña Siegfrieda. But yet
he could not remember his combustible
wedding night. Shortly thereafter her teutonic
buxom body was a wan ache, remote as some
snow-fed star.

How could he account for the threadbare
ennui of their conjugal bed that at first had been
in his cinnabar voluptuous nostrils.
Momentarily, he thought of Lais's glabrous
skin. Then he fell into a fruitless prate and he
idly wondered who was the person fulfilled by
his discourse. "What Theban towers I had
ruined, and how many sable sails I had plied in
Ceylon."

Doña Siegfrieda was buried at noon; pure,
she was impervious to the cormorant animal
sun that feeds on profligate flies.

The entire town wept. No Hay Nada was a
silver chalice for the nacreous tears of the bereft
folks. Why were the natives broken in pieces?

Pack-penny Nature had erred: the wrong person was buried. Long as Don Pablo declined to enter the nether world, his anxious beneficiaries were denied their just reward.

A troop of becrazed women, with ashes strewn upon their waspish hair and skirts lifted, ran through Calle la Luna and past the Plaza Bartolomé. They were scaly furies, one panegyrizing the chastity of Doña Siegfrieda's gallinaceous brood, another demanding that as a memorial to her alabaster virtues, a pissing conduit be built. One, in hugger-mugger, accused Don Pablo of pillaging sylphs as if they were cities famed for their aromatic gums.

Midday, Dolly was in the orange grove holding a watch in his hand as the water flowed from the Majorcan mountains down through the *huerta* into the parched clay vale. Once a week, water ran through the cement channels in the orchards.

Pablo was motionless in his curule chair, his steep brows a cemetery of mute sorrow.

Patch was about to go to Biniaraix to an outdoor dirt café for cognac. He stayed his impulse to study Pablo's weather-headed changes, wondering if he would receive a

pittance of his goods and chattels. Dolly rushed
towards Don Pablo, kissed the tattered sleeve of
his jerkin, pressed his lips against the latchet of
one shoe, and begged his brother: "My pockets
are barren as Rachel, whilst yours are rank and
fat as the plains of Gennesareth. Lest I perish,
give me, I pray, a farthing of your foison
abundant as Herod's palms Cleopatra coveted."

Don Pablo: "You'll not melt the musky core
of my heart."

Dolly: "Is not a sage like you a marmoreal
wonder?"

Don Pablo: "Perhaps I've had some
clandestine need of a shack like you. I suppose
I've accepted your withered foibles because it
raises my self-esteem. Don't simper, Patch. A
smirk is often a deeper gash in the flesh than
the blade of a bodkin."

Dolly: "You've been a virid widower for
forty-eight hours; am I to be vomited forth once
more for your moribund genitories?"

Don Pablo: "I am a bond servant in my
unwombed Egypt crying out for the leeks, the
cucumbers, and the garlic of a woman's spiced
skirts."

Dolly: "I've never been your caterpillar like

Leandro who cozened you soon as he was your hireling."

Don Pablo: "Cheating is a Levantine custom. That swart Arabic countenance that resembles a calabash entertains me. His father gives five pesetas each year to the patron of his trade, St. Onorato, who guards bakers, and his uncle offers seven pesetas annually to Santa Carmen, who sees to it that the fishers have a bountiful harvest at sea. Leandro's father and uncle were forced by a troop of falangists to swallow an earthen vase of motor oil.

"I won't return to English Kent: Yea, my feet are ashy as the roots of a dotard olive which is green and flowering at its top. Long ago I knew that lust is a sciatica provided by Eros."

Dolly: "What know you how an anchor or a quadrant is wrought? You peddled flatirons from door to door at Kent; then you were a drummer for kerosene stoves in the Midlands. Afterwards a chapman, and your wares were old skillets, skewers, saucepans, and kitchen spatulas. You fell into one lewd trade after another to stew over female gauds, trinkets, and their cinnamon underwear: corset-covers, chemises, shifts, and nightgowns. Your

commerce was lechery. You became a
proprietor of a dry goods store filled with
women's hosiery, pins, needles, threads, cotton
knickers, buttons, lace, pink drawers, pomade;
nothing was such a relish as helping a
smoldering matron get into a pair of bedroom
slippers and patent leather shoes. Should she
smell of a back-house, she was your most
toothsome confection."

Don Pablo: "Nature was my lecherous
teacher."

Dolly: "Now just departing the leafy July of
my age, I don't paint my visage or use a daub to
hide my roaring envy of your regal largess;
though your sable tillage in all fecund countries
entombed my hopes. I was undone as a child.
Mother mistook my timorous carriage,
regarding me a misbegotten dolt. Of course, I
always was ill-prepared for your riffraff ort of
cavil. A guileless, fallow young man, I esteemed
another man's wife and mistrusted your illicit
levity; for I would as lief enter an enshrined
womb as be a housebreaker. Parse your carnal
syntax and clause a calvish apotheosis of a
cranny between the vagrant legs of any shrew. I
watched you drink up a mercer's cloth, divers

fabrics, cambric, linsey-woolsey, of lubricious
widows as though you were a tireless sot. Did
our blessed Mother teach you to skelder?"

Don Pablo: "Half of my origins were yours;
but I swore at Ill-Luck, determined to leave
behind me the babbles, the botch of ills, and the
sour pukes of a mud puppy, and after cleaning
cuspidors in a mug-house of Coventry for a year
was a seaman on a freighter laden with English
coal and bound for Ceylon. Supposing I
couldn't eschew misfortune, my supper would
have been reeds, bark, tropical gales, humid sea
wind.

"I had an intrigue with a marvelous
bay-haired minx and from her I got my first
windfall, gonorrhea, and then dysentery. So
once more I was a sailor in a carrack returning
to Plymouth, where I found a job as a porter in
the stews. The wenches were civil and I
managed to buy and hawk flannel camisoles,
Canton damasks, bedpans for pregnant crones,
girdles, pin cushions, face powder with which I
massaged the supple legs of parlor maids. I got
enough pound sterling from an Irish Catholic
petticoat for the imported ashes of Golgotha.
Once more in Ceylon, it looked as if

God-fearing Evil Tidings always was at my side
until I met a mulatto who purchased a goatskin
from me filled with Mohamet's visions. Then I
bought a tiny forest of cork trees, and a leaky
caravel that contained a store of India pepper,
resin gums, and Carib quaiacum that I mixed
with surgical spirits to releave unwed waitresses
of heart-balm. Thereafter, I rented a stall at
Marseilles where I sold Cana vessels of the
living waters to a bawdy bishop. With the
money from that I purchased ten thousand vats
of Egyptian beer brewed at the time of the
Exodus and got rid of that to a Gentile
money-lender who wore a Rabbinic beard. By
now I was climbing Jacob's Ladder and
succeeded as an antiquarian by collecting or
digging up the wimple of Poppaea, the codpiece
of usurious Seneca, the tire of Aspasia, the
whore of Pericles. The antique articles brought
me eight garners of wheat, barley, and oats I
hawked at robber prices to the people in Cairo
during a bread-famine. I also received for
Joseph's Coat of Many Colors three houses
outside Alexandria, and the purchaser was so
overjoyed that I gave him as a bonus a bit of
marble of Christ's sepulchre as well as one inch

of his footprints. Then three men from
Damascus, proprietors of several brothels in
various parcels of Syria, relieved me of eight
night-shifts worn by Mary Magdalene in the
public stews of Tyre. I skipped town before
they discovered they came from the factories of
Manchester. My riches grew big as
Behemoth."

Dolly: "Does one Sabine virgin remain since
Latium was ravaged? Brother, you are old, old,
and older than old, and no longer does your
canorous blood cry out for a chine of saffron
skin.

"How can you bombast your bones, blind,
hoary Tiresias?"

Don Pablo: "The gods themselves, not equal
to the power of Nature, grow weary of their
ancient groins."

Dolly: "Heed this exhortation: Hector always
left the bed of Andromeda before battling the
Argives, and fell not at the feral hands of
Achilles, but into the womb of his Trojan
spouse. I laugh at your scrubby triumphs, your
oily addle swoons, and your infantine mischief
with weather-headed slovens. A junket or julep
to you has never been savory to me. I'm frank,

with no clandestine pang for your vestal Celtic kite.

"A maiden, hankering for constant virtue, ought to preserve it from spoil by building a stone wall around it, aside from several parapets, the towers of ancient Jerusalem, as well as a moat. Lais, similar to the coward Britons, when Julius Caesar arrived, has little to defend her blush except a thin woodland and a ditch.

"The most sinister adversary to a maiden's modesty is her husband's bosom friend who at the start desires to be chosen as his companion's consort; then her groom is neighing at his wife who is vain, assuming her own consort, enfeebled by age and cloying habit, is prepared to defile the marriage-bed. In a brace of years the spouse is sure her lien is impotent, or indifferent as her mirror. Be vigilant, O husband, since fornication is a subtle cognomen for perfidy, falsehood, and a common pickpurse of your wife's secret parts.

"When it's February in the Balearics my almonds flower and my few rustic vices are Catonian buds. In the September downpour, I'm distempered. Sure, I'm a dull witling, but never somebody else. I hear Lais has loitered in Amsterdam, Paris, and Birmingham; she goes here and there much the same way as she rummages in Spanish villages, but toying with rake-hell waiters, scavengers."

Don Pablo: "What sickens you is you really think you're different each day. You try to outwit grizzled Proteus. An original man is rain, sleet, snow, frost, and hailstones, and all in one caitiff hour. That's why Abel doesn't know how to handle your novel style of behavior."

Don Pablo's ire grew: "How your wild garbaged nose has spread among the rubbish heap of your face, sometimes the color of spinach and then of garlic. Is the boiling spleen in one eye equal to the filthy bile in the other? Am I likely to be undone by your apish chat?

"Abel comes here as if he were lame, blind, and palsied, hoping you might lave his imaginary infirmities in your Pool of Bethesda. Besides, you're a miserable poseur of a human being."

Dolly: "What right have you to frolic with my affectations?"

Don Pablo: "None, except that I lodge, feed, fuel, and willy-nilly, stuff them."

Dolly: "Am I to fare no better than Hagar and her bastard Ishmael, to be cast out with a cruse of water and yesterday's Majorcan crust of bread? Or to lie prone before your shoes and chomp their leather, or diet upon an orphaned shoelace?"

Don Pablo's mind was a hilly tract of breccia, and he sat, vowing to damnify Antonio Mentira. How short a space could he expect his betrothed Lais to wear the garb of lamentation? Once she took off her callow weed, who then would succor his grieving headstone? "Suppose the Notary Public of Palma is minded to chew the skirts, dresses, the linen shifts of my turtledove, who'll howl for my gewgaw bones? The grave's a furnace of boiling jibes and flouts. How provide Lais with battlements, turrets, ramparts, and the Walls of Jerusalem so that no vermin Titus can lay siege to her blush? No one of my wintery, hoary name, shall be an ointment for a Majorcan insect. Should a Catalan pimp enter her inn I'll posthumously blast the 10,000 frankincense trees in Arabia Felix, my entire shares of the Cunard Line, the securities I hold of Sheffield steel, and foreclose every *finca* at Formentor, Biniarix, Puerto de

Pollensa, nine Catholic nunneries, thirteen
well-timbered church porches, seventy houses
of ill-fame, and two museum synagogues, one in
Cordoba, the other, Toledo."

Several pebble tears fell out of his shrunken
eyes, and unmindful of his gender, he thought
he was Lilith who lay with Adam and conceived
and bare stones.

Mercedes genuflected, then gave him the
daily rag, *Baleares.* He sampled the obituaries,
then blessed the loins of Abraham, Isaac, and
Jacob, as he came upon his own death notice
and read: "Sir Pablo Williams, never a certified
member of the human race, expired with a rare,
ill-starred disease, lately discovered by notable
alchemists as Kindness."

Then Don Pablo shouted: "I'm dead, and I
know it!"

Dolly whining, who had drunk twelve glasses
of cognac, tartly answered: "Woe is all flesh.
You are still alive."

Don Pablo shook his fist at Dolly: "One
more testimonial from you and I'll leave you
the cony that ravaged Spain when the Roman
legions ruled the land."

There was a shifty gorgan in Dolly's eye.

Suddenly, he jumped up and down on Pablo's
pained, arthritic feet. Pablo winced, but
grasping a water carafe next him, broke it
against Dolly's face. The blood rang as it ran
out of Dolly's blubbered eyes and covered his
jaw with vermillion gore.

Dolly cursed him: "Spoiler of the ointment
of the chaste conjugal couch!"

Pablo struck him with his fist, and the
wilderness animal in Dolly howled. Pablo spat
upon him: "Was I not always your Pelian ash,
knowing you were spawned in our mother's
lewd boiling sheets? You sapped the larder and
the timbers of my house and swallowed my
cellar. You're a cyclone of ill tidings.

"You devoured my inward crops. Get out;
drink your cup of spittle as your cordial and let
my mind wander and nuzzle for the milky paps
of the Hellespont. Find a bed in a cleft betwixt
two rocks; eat cockle and chew noisome weeds,
and at eventide bolt down Charles's Wain."

For several days Patch's food was the
horsehair and wool inside his pallet.

Dolly knelt, begging Don Pablo for a small
bowl of porridge; but Pablo was mute.

Dolly Patch hurried to No Hay Nada to enter into a discourse with El Medico, *Abogado* Mentira, and the Proprietor of El Colmado.

El Medico stroked Dolly's brooding neck, the Proprietor of El Colmado la Luna gave him sweetmeat to cocker him and Don Bartolomé suddenly awoke: "Could you believe that in my youth I was needy as Hunger?"

Dolly, tears fogging his eyes, blurted forth: "Don Pablo has an iron resolve not to flit out of his life. He venerates the Patriarch of the Old Testament who begat Isaac at one hundred years of age. If he has a mild, salubrious hour he asserts he's good as Seth. By prime noon, he misprizes Arphaxad who begat at his thirty-fifth year Salah."

Abogado Mentira posing as an haruspex was prophetic: "He'll attend our funerals and consider our wakes and vigils a voluptuous riot. He remains alive only to trifle with our *pesetas,* merchandise, orchards, and God Himself."

Don Bartolomé joined the lamentation: "Long before our bodies shall be the forfeit of Christ, the groves, houses, gardens, pears, almonds, everything we own, will be gone, and the gossips will say, 'Observe the four giddy goats who were pocketed by the lion, Don Pablo.' "

Then there was an outcry from the Proprietor of El Colmado la Luna: "I'm already asleep in my urn. The Saint has bolted down my seven windmills at El Molinar, 200,000 *pesetas* worth of *paella* and twelve harvests of almonds from my orchard in Murcia."

Dolly: "The Saint is mad enough without seven windmills blowing about his head. He's fickle as the lee tide, running against the wind."

Abogado Mentira: "Where is the testament he wanted to borrow to enlarge his bequests for my bridal day although I've been a married householder for a generation? Soon as I'm dead he'll ravish all my savings at *Hispano Americano*. I also donated Chopin's piano at Valldemosa to Don Pablo; of course, it's a fraud, for all the keys are white as a leper.

"I thought we were besieging Villa D'Or while he was routing us. I had hoped to retire to the monastery at Vallbona and be rich and pious as Carlos the Fifth." *Abogado* Mentira's tongue was dry, smarted and salted as if it were being prepared for the table.

El Medico: "The Ancient One is the same as the juice of myrtle leaves, for after they are pithless and sere they stink like any dead body. The paradox remains: How can he smell like a carrion Majorcan mongrel and still be void of a winding sheet?"

Don Bartolomé's fat heart fell: "Jesus, Mary, and Joseph, he'll take my dwellings in El Terreno, C'an Bernadette at S'aroca, and three *fincas* at Maramar, all dear to my Samaritan breast as the host in the monstrance."

Abogado Mentira: "There's that wheezing notary in No Hay Nada, and the Grand Notary Public in Palma who have added divers solemn emendations that are as orgulous as a great pedant's footnote, likely concealed beneath a housemaid's floor cloth in Bunyola."

Dolly: "How frequently I've been the prey of his upbraids I suspected were the sole vent of his wild, bilious age. I've drowned my umbrage rigorous as Rhadamanthus's judgments in the lower realm, seeing that he was a thrall to a shrewish bog. I beseeched him to leave her a pelting jointure, so that for more than a moiety of his infinite shares, stocks, and pounds sterling would be bequeathed to the Father,

Son, and Holy Ghost: El Medico, Don
Bartolomé, and *Abogado* Antonio Mentira. O
El Medico, medicine this bedlamite, lest we be
roving vagabonds in the dispeopled streets
within us."

El Medico: "My Sacred Brothers, let us not
raise up a pother. On the morrow, I'll farce this
fraudulent Titan with a twilight supper of dwarf
furze, four ounces of Mallorquin sewage
sprinkled with a boar's urine, a pimiento
dressed with a guinea-worm and swamp
nitrates. Before the moon sheds its marmoreal
snows upon *Puig Major,* we'll be the landlords
of the Balearics, Iberia, the Midi, and our
Canarias."

Instead of the fatal physic El Medico was to
supply Don Pablo, he gave him an immoderate
infusion of fleawort which maddens the brain.

Don Pablo's midnight head was the breviary
of his dole and drought.

El Medico, beside himself, gave Don Pablo a
remedy that was another windstorm in the aged
man's rueful cranium. Who seeds one's failures
save men; lunatic Alexander of Macedon was
advised not to conquer Scythia, since he only
would be ravaging poverty.

Lais O'Shea appeared, and El Medico,
posing as Don Pablo's guardian, begged her not
to be a nest of wasps to his expiring patient.
Suddenly he genuflected and said: "Virgin
Mary, do not step upon Don Pablo's antique
nerves or his blood that's torn asunder." And
then El Medico went away.

Don Pablo suddenly moved and parted his
half-dead lips: "Why do you eat my grief as a
mastiff drinking a puddle of a hare's entrails?
You yielded up the Holy Ghost of one week I
need. Where were your maidenly footsteps?
Should my widow imbibe the mouthed brewage
of my moorish man-servant, Leandro?

"I abide by the feral greed of Bartolomé,
waters that breed duckweed, but is this holy
Catholic incense? You come here with void
arms spiritless as the sandstone cathedral at
Palma. Are you empty as the Gothic ribs of that
church? Could you not be steadfast until my
bones dwell in the marshes of woeful Avernus?
Are your figure, clothes, feet whets for booby
workmen? Bred up in Catholic precepts, were
you a comfit swallowed up in stews no larger
than a trencher?"

Don Pablo continued: "I realize Truth, a

lonely, bizarre fellow rambling in the wilderness
of city curbstones, wholly bemused, is the
victim of brawny bulls ranging the streets. Each
man is a brute ready to devour his gibbets of
backhouse dogmas he pretends is pragmatical
light. Still, are you a hackney or chaste?"

Lais: "Sir Pablo, though I was at a
hedge-school for a short while, I don't
understand your hard words; are they lame,
perhaps too wrinkled and aged for me to have
learnt them?"

Don Pablo admitted he was no gospell'd
carping fellow and always had been an adulterer
neighing at a grease-bellied slattern, and he
would not daub his lewd fires to marry Lais
O'Shea: "Since I know not who I am, you can
anticipate a causeless thunderclap of spleen; or,
if the skies are blowsy, an unlook'd for quip.
Really, I'm a wag in all sorts of weather.
Though I'm unwed, I hear I'm a cuckold, or
am I like the wittol Roman emperor Galba? All
this is a muddled study in First Causes."

Lais: "Sir, what's a cuckold?"

Don Pablo: "A unicorn has one horn. Were
it doubled, it could be fatal to marriage as
hemlock.

"Though I'm perverse as the four seasons, I can say yea or nay. I am far less vigilant than a caterpillar; I have the lubricious eyes of Argus in my back, and somehow guess if your body is rye-grass for a drayman. Was Antonio Mentira's breath ever close to your untamed country mouth?"

Lais: "No, sir. Don Antonio smells bad."

There was a chink in Don Pablo's tallow face that resembled a smile, but he blasted her with contumely: "Be bleak and frigid with the Catalonian born under the sign of watery Hyades. He's dour, but seminal in the rain. Avoid an Andalusian; his star is Pisces, the exsanguinous fish, but he adores the feminine harp and sackbut of canorous billows."

He stroked her blazing red hair with his numb fingers. "There are maidservants whose kennel effluvium attracts any riggish fly."

Don Pablo went on: "At Sidon, in my virgin prime, King Hiram furnished me with 3,000 men to hew my timbers. When I was in Barbados, I was a freebooter, buying and selling tall, willowy black slaves. Then I became a shipbuilder in Plymouth. I studied the silvery and sable triremes of the Romans. Had I been

at Actium when perfidious, warty Cleopatra fled
with her sixty sails, I still could have vanquished
Boy Octavius Augustus Caesar. I can carve in
my head the littoral towns of Sparta. For gaudy
cosmetics, lipstick, eye shadow you'll be the
mistress of the sweet-peopled towns of Grecian
Cardamille, Enope, and Hyla. For your girdles,
golden hairpins, ermines, unguent, capes, silver,
platinum, you'll govern Anthaea, Epea, and
wine-flowing Pedassus. Let me twine my gone
life around your waist, and the hour after our
wedlock I'll be in Erebus and you the sovereign
of unimaginable fables."

Lais was as enigmatic as the Sibylline books.

In the meantime El Medico had no choice
than to be the spagyric chef of the Last Supper
for the Ancient One.

Abel beheld El Medico holding up his
whelked belly as he leaned on his squab legs.
Abel hurried towards him as El Medico
attempted to shamble along Calle la Luna. El
Medico stumbled and fell.

"O Sir El Medico, you too are a mountebank
Luke unable to cure a crotchet in your head."

El Medico: "Harebrain, step aside. I'll never

have any time for you until I'm in Apocalyptic
Paradise. I'm always late; everything is tardy
except misfortune."

Abel interrupted: "A fellow with clothes he
must have bought at a slop shop knocked on my
door announcing himself as the Honorable
Good Hap. Certain he was a poseur, I shut the
door against his face."

El Medico: "Pest, *Abogado* Mon Honneur
awaits me."

Abel exclaimed: "Is there an *Abogado* Mon
Honneur on a pettifogger's throne between
archangels Michael and Gabriel?"

El Medico: "Don't drumble; are you a
pedagogue who doesn't know that *Abogado*
Mon Honneur is his foul Excellency Antonio
Mentira? But I must run, flee, gallop. What's
your most recent affliction?"

Abel: "Sir El Medico, last night I dreamt I
had a bad breath."

El Medico: "Breathe hard and come next to
me."

Abel: "Dear El Medico, my nose already flits
away because it cannot endure me."

El Medico: "You have a salubrious mouth,
but if you are convinced you smell bad, who can

remedy you? I'm really in a rush, but I tell you again, I can't smell you at all.

"Go to the apothecary and ask for the buds of hops with wine boiled in a pipkin. Should you still assume you are a carrier of the filth in our summer *torrente,* then ask for *Ramunculus aquatilis* to physic your swashy trances."

Abel: "I beseech you, kind El Medico, at this instant as my tongue reaches my dry palate, and as I open my gulfy mouth, I imagine my stench is worse than offal."

El Medico: "There's a tornado of noisome ills in your pate. Are your gut, bladder, kidney, and sacrum shrunk together? There's a whirlpool in your pericranium. Visit the shrine and remains of Benedict Biscop. I can't recall a saint who holds a crozier who might alleviate your plight."

Abel: "Did these saints die of their own rotten ordure? Is one corrupt scent an antidote to another?"

El Medico vanished and Abel stood smelling himself.

El Medico was in his surgery. His pelican sat on a burner into which he cast leaves of nightshade, the core of a wild apple he had sowed in the dung of a burro, a dram of an old hag mixed with sea grape, honey figs, and ten grams of white hellebore.

At Villa D'Or, Don Pablo, imbibing the soft Iberian sky, swallowed El Medico's brew. His funeral was fantastical; the hearse was decked with bougainvillaea and the Tears of the Virgin.

The will was without a flaw, with one exception. Don Pablo had entertained so many wives, courtesans, and secondhand virgins, that all he left was Villa D'Or and a pile of dodkins, the inheritance of a fifteenth-century galley merchant from Genova, hidden somewhere in the ground underneath the chicken wire.

Following the day of Don Pablo's demise the villagers set it aside as twenty-four hours of lamentation. Unlike Herod's command that every Hebrew infant be slain so that it might appear that fathers, mothers, brothers, and sisters mourned the death of their Edomite king, the natives wept because Percival Williams' bequest to the town was *no hay nada*.

Dolly Patch expired in Kent a year later. Not Lot's wife, Lais O'Shea did not pine away for her past since she never shed enough tears to become a pillar of salt.

Abel returned to New York and by then knew he had to relinquish the herbs and the purges he hoped would give him a milder disposition. After fifty years as a noddy, he was so gorged with amazing proverbs, adages, saws, homilies, psalms, that it was clear he would never be any better than he was and that was bad enough.

Selah.